哈福

哈福

哈福

7天學好 Talk a lot in English

流利英語會話

會話‧聽力‧口說，一學就會
英文會話速成66公式，10倍速流利脫口說

 附 MP3　施孝昌◎著

分分秒秒，直覺英語，聽力好！會話好！

1效	輕鬆-釋放聽說，英語的膽量	4效	會話聽力急速攀升
2效	自然-誘發口耳，聽說的能力	5效	從會話提升英聽力
3效	直接-快速搶攻，外語的版圖	6效	從聽力強化英會話

超強英語學習書，迫不及待成為英語高手

我們的任務是使每位學英語的人，都能「學最純正、最常用的英語！」所以，本書的對話，都是生活中自然純正的美式英語會話，跟著學習，自然可以隨時隨地流利說出，連老外都說讚的英語。

英文會話速成 66 公式
10 倍速流利英語快可說

　　學英語的年齡層逐漸降低，英語已成為國際溝通的共通語言，大部分人在接受完整的國家教育階段，雖然能夠將英語背得滾瓜爛熟，卻不見得有把握把英語學得巧、聽得懂、說得好。許多人往往學了 10 年英語還是聽不懂、不會說；學了多年的英語，一旦碰到外國人，才知道只會說「Hello!」、「Good morning!」。

　　那是因為從小到大，我們在學校所學的是英語的「知識」，而非英語的「說法」，偏重讀與寫，忽略聽與說，一旦過了學語言的黃金塑造期後，想要突破膽量，開口說英語，卻礙於語言的思考已固著於文法結構，因此才無法順暢、輕鬆地用簡單的口語表達出來。

　　學習者往往一逕加強英文讀寫，卻忘了「說」英語才是人們溝通最頻繁的渠道。目前外界雖然有許多語言補習班，但也因其皆有教學進度，無法配合個人的學習速度，往往難收實質效果，徒然浪費金錢。

　　「聽」與「說」總是相輔相成的，學語言最重要的還是

要選一本適合自己的教材，能夠配合自己的時間，反覆聽標準 CD 訓練聽力的敏銳度，並且大聲朗誦、大聲對話，甚至可以自己錄下來，矯正發音，掌握英語的節奏與速度，很快你就會驚覺耳道暢通到地球村囉！

本書皆為道地的生活化用語，從頭至尾沒有一個難字，本書內容共分 10 章，66 個單元實用會話，是英文會話速成的 66 個黃金公式，讓您 10 倍速流利脫口說。內含示範對話、情境對話、例句隨身包三個主要部分。結合生活＆保健、求職＆理財，編輯內容涵蓋生活各個層面，收錄多方面場合之常用語，讓英語學習更為貼近生活的需要。

尤其對於想出國留學、在海外定居、或想使英語會話更進步的族群，讓你最直接搶攻英語版圖，最快速擷取精華養分，是一本非常便利的工具書。

另外也有專業標準發音 CD 及配樂，讓讀者可以邊聽邊說，增進口語及聽力實力，輕鬆釋放你說英語的膽量，自然誘發你的外語口說能力，讓你停滯不前的英語，急速攀升，成為最具競爭力的 E 人類！

Contents

Chapter 5 保健英語

Part 1 Going to See a Doctor 看醫生

Contents

Contents

Chapter 9 投資理財

Contents

Chapter 10 求救！

Chapter 1

電話英語

你有過這樣的經驗嗎？

　　一接起電話，卻聽到對方霹哩啪啦講著一大串的英語……，當時的你是應付自如，還是張口結舌，不知所措呢？現在就打開「樂透話匣子」，馬上幫你克服和老外講電話的恐懼，讓你的職場生涯如魚得水。

Unit

1

MP3-2

Making Phone Calls
打電話

示範對話

1

A Pizza Hut. This is Tommy.
Can I help you?

B Yes, I would like to order two large cheese pizzas.

> **A** 必勝客，我是湯米。
> 有什麼可以為您服務的嗎？
> **B** 是的，我想點兩個大的起司披薩。

2

A Hello, Smith residence.

B Hi. I am calling in response to the ad in the newspaper on Friday.
I understand you're selling kittens?

> **A** 嗨，史密斯公館。
> **B** 嗨，我看到星期五報紙上的廣告，所以打電話過來。
> 你們有小貓要賣是嗎？

情境對話

A Red Lobster. Can I help you?
紅龍蝦餐廳，有什麼可以為您服務的嗎？

B Hi. I would like to make a reservation for tomorrow evening.
嗨，我想要預約明天晚上。

A Okay. What time would you like to make that?
好的，您想預約幾點？

B Seven o'clock.
七點。

A And how many people would this be for?
請問有幾個人呢？

B Twenty. We are having a birthday party.
20 個人，我們要開生日派對。

❶ May I speak to John, please?
麻煩一下，我找約翰。

❷ Is this United Nations Bank?
請問你那邊是「聯合國家銀行」嗎？

❸ Hello. I need to place an order, please.
嗨，我要下單。

❹ Can I make a doctor's appointment with Dr. Lee for tomorrow, please?
我能否和李醫生預約明天？

❺ I need to speak to a manager.
我需要和經理談談。

I left my purse at your restaurant.
我把皮包掉在你們的餐廳了。

Unit

2

MP3-3

Directory Assistance
請接線生幫忙

示範對話

1

A Thank you for choosing Southwestern Bell. How can I help you?

B I need the phone number for Northpark Elementary School, please.

   A 謝謝您使用西南貝爾的服務。
       有什麼可以協助您的地方嗎？
   B 我需要北園國小的電話號碼，麻煩一下。

2

A Operator. What city, please?

B Dallas.

   A 接線中心，請問您要查號的城市？
   B 達拉斯。

3

A I need the number for a movie theater in Irving.

B What street?

A 我要查艾文市一家電影院的電話。
B 請問那裡的街名為何？

4

A I am looking for the number to a movie theater at the Irving exit 12 in Irving.

B I'm sorry. There isn't a listing for a movie theater at that location.

A 艾文市在艾文 12 號出口處有家電影院，我要查那裡的電話號碼，
B 很抱歉，那個地點沒有登記任何電影院。

5

A Could you give me the number for a restaurant near the highway and Main St.?

B Any restaurant? Or did you have a particular one in mind?

A 靠近高速公路和緬因街的餐廳，能否幫我查一下電話號碼？
B 任何一家嗎？還是你有特定的餐廳名稱？

6

A Will there be long-distance charges?

B No, it is a metro number.

A 這是長途電話嗎？

B 不是，這是市內電話。

情境對話

A Thank you for choosing Southwestern Bell.
謝謝您使用西南貝爾的服務。

How can I help you?
有什麼可以為您服務的嗎？

B I need the number for Mr. Nick Russell on Cherry Tree Lane.
我要查尼克羅素的電話號碼，他住在櫻桃樹街。

A That is Russell with two l's, right?
羅素先生的名字有兩個 L，對不對？

B Yes. R-U-S-S-E-L-L.
是的，拼法是 R-U-S-S-E-L-L。

A Nick Russell on 1234 Cherry Tree Lane. Hold for the number please.

尼克羅素的地址是櫻桃樹街 1234 號，請等一下，我馬上為您查他的電話號碼。

B Thank you.

謝謝。

例句隨身包

❶ The number is 555-4321, repeating 555-4321.

您要查的電話號碼是 555-4321，重複一遍 555-4321。

To automatically dial this number at extra charge, push "one" now.

如果要自動轉接的話，會額外收取費用，要的話請按「1」。

❷ The area code for that number has changed.

那個電話號碼的區域碼已經改了。

It is no longer considered to be in Dallas but in Denton.

不再用達拉斯的區域號碼，而是用丹頓的區域號碼了。

Unit

3

MP3-4

Answering the Phone
應答電話

 示範對話

1

A This is Keri. Can I help you?
B I am not sure. I may have the wrong number. I need to get a hold of Jimmy.

A 我是凱莉，有什麼可以為您服務的嗎？
B 我不太確定，我可能打錯電話了。
我需要聯絡吉米。

2

B Thank you for calling Montgomery Wards. This is Amy.
A Hello. I have a question regarding my credit card bill.
B Okay. Please hold while I redirect you to customer service.

B 謝謝您來電蒙哥馬利百貨公司，我是艾咪。
A 嗨，我有一個關於信用卡帳單的問題。
B 好的，請稍等，我將幫您接通客服部。

A Hello.
哈囉。

B May I speak to Kevin please?
我找凱文。

A Speaking.
我就是。

B Kevin? This is Pamela.
凱文嗎？我是潘蜜拉。

Did you get my message?
你接到我的留言了嗎？

A No. Why?
沒有，怎麼了嗎？

Did you need something?
妳需要什麼東西嗎？

B Yes. I need someone to come in and work next Tuesday.
是的，我下星期二需要找人進辦公室上班。

例句隨身包

❶ John speaking.
我是約翰。

❷ Hello. Dr. Makler's office.
嗨，這裡是麥可勒醫生辦公室。

❸ Gonzales residence.
岡澤拉公館。

❹ Holiday Inn. How can I direct your call?
假日旅館，請問您要找哪位？

❺ Kizer Enterprises. This is Jason speaking.
克石企業，我是傑森。

How may I help you?
有什麼可以為您服務的嗎？

23

Wrong Number
撥錯電話號碼

示範對話

1

A Can I speak to Mr. Ken Lakeshore please?

B Sorry, you have the wrong number.

    A 我找肯恩胡岸先生？

    B 抱歉，你打錯了。

2

A You must have the wrong number.
This is the Kenshire residence.

B Sorry to bother you. Goodbye.

    A 妳一定是打錯了。
       這裡是肯社公館。

    B 很抱歉打擾您，再見。

A Hello? Pamela, is that you?

B No. There is no one who lives here by that name.
You must have the wrong number.

3

  A 嗨，妳是潘蜜拉嗎？

  B 不是，這裡沒有這個人。
妳一定是打錯號碼了。

A Is Jack there?

B No, you can only reach him here after seven.
Why don't you try his office number?

4

  A 傑克在嗎？

  B 他不在，他只有七點以後才會在這裡。
你可以打電話到他辦公室去。

A Is this the home of Mikeal L. McKingley?

B No. Wrong number.
He moved out last month.

5

  A 您那邊是米契爾麥肯利的家嗎？

  B 不是，你打錯了。
他上個月搬走了。

A Is this 530-8634?

B No. You have the wrong number.
This is 520-8634.

    A 您那邊是 530-8634 嗎？
    B 不是，你打錯電話號碼了。
        這裡的電話是 520-8634。

6

A I am trying to get a hold of Wendy. Is she there?

B Wendy? No, you must have the wrong number.
There is no one named Wendy who lives here.

    A 我要找溫蒂，她在嗎？
    B 溫蒂？你一定是打錯了。
        這裡沒有溫蒂這個人。

7

情境對話

A Hello.
嗨。

B Hello. My name is Greg Abott.
嗨，我是葛瑞克阿罷。

Is Jason Marshall there?
請問傑森瑪索在嗎？

A No. You have the wrong number.
你打錯電話了。

B This is not the Marshall's number anymore?
這個不再是瑪索家的電話號碼了嗎？

A I think you dialed the wrong number.
我想你可能撥錯號碼了。

We have lived here for twenty-eight years.
我們已經在這裡住了 28 年了。

B Thanks for your time.
謝謝。

Sorry to bother you.
打擾到你，真是不好意思。

Unit

5

MP3-6

Taking Messages
幫你留言

 示範對話

1

A Hello. Is Katie there?

B Sorry, she won't be back until late this evening. May I take a message?

A 嗨,凱蒂在嗎?
B 抱歉,她要到晚一點才會回來。
要不要留話?

2

A I need to speak with Mrs. Weigel. Is she there?

B Yes. However, she is with a client right now. May I take a message?

A 我想找魏格太太。
她在嗎?
B 她在,但她現在正在和客戶交談。
我可以幫你留言嗎?

3

A May I take a message? He is busy right now.

B Yes. Please tell him that Kim called and needs a copy of his tax report.

  A 你要留話嗎？他現在正在忙。

  B 好的，請告訴他京姆打電話來過，我需要他的報稅影本。

4

A Can you tell her that Aaron called?

B Yes. Is there any other message I should leave for her?

  A 麻煩你告訴她艾倫來過電話？

  B 好的，你還要我轉達她其他的話嗎？

5

A I am sorry. Mr. Hannon can't come to the phone right now.
I would be happy to take a message.

B No, thanks. I will just call back later.

  A 抱歉，瀚能先生現在無法接聽。
我可以幫你留言。

  B 謝謝，不用了，我待會再打電話過來。

6

A I will have to take a message.
She is unavailable right now.

B Just tell her that Sherry called, please.

    A 我得幫你留個話。
       她現在沒空。
    B 請告訴她雪莉來過電話。

7

A I am sorry. The manager just left.
May I get your phone number and name
and have him call you back?

B No, that's fine. I will just call back later.

    A 很抱歉,經理剛剛離開。
       可以請你留個電話、姓名,我再請他回電,好嗎?
    B 不用了,沒關係,我待會再打電話過來。

8

A Let me just write down your name and
number.
Mr. Hopkins will call you back as soon as he
can.

B Great. Thanks.

    A 讓我寫下你的姓名和電話。
       哈普金斯先生會盡快給您回電。
    B 太棒了,謝謝。

情境對話

A Hi. Is Candi Smith there?
嗨，肯蒂史密斯在嗎？

B No. I am sorry. I will have to take a message.
抱歉，她不在，我只能幫你留言。

A Okay. Just tell her Gene Arnold called.
好的，告訴她吉妮阿諾來過電話。

B Sure. That was Gene Arnold, right?
沒問題，你是吉妮阿諾的，對吧？

A Yes. That is correct.
是的，沒錯。

Can you please tell her that it's urgent?
你能不能告訴她我有急事？

B Of course. I will get the message to her as soon as she arrives.
沒問題，她一到，我就會把你的留言給她。

Unit

6

MP3-7

Asking the Other Party to Talk Slower

請對方講慢一點.

示範對話

1

A Can you please tell him Mr. Samuel J. Johnston called please.

B Sorry, can you please talk slower? I didn't quite catch your name.

    A 你能否告訴他山姆強森來過電話。

    B 抱歉，你能不能講慢一點？
       我沒有聽清楚你的名字。

2

A Could you repeat the message, please? I didn't get the entire message.

B Yes. Maybe if I talked slower, it would help.

    A 你能否再重複一次留言內容？
       我沒聽到整個內容。

    B 好的，也許我說慢一點，會比較好。

A Could you talk slower?
Now, whom are you trying to reach?

3

B I need to speak to Jerry Morgan.
It is urgent!

A 你可以說慢一點嗎？
請問你要找哪一位？

B 我需要和傑瑞摩根談談。
我有急事。

A Could you repeat your message and talk
slower and clearer?
I don't think I wrote it down right.

4

B Just tell him Ann called.
will talk to him about the rest when he
calls me.

A 你能否重複一下留言內容，說話速度可以慢一點嗎？
我不確定自己剛剛記下的是對的。

B 告訴他安來過電話就可以了。
當他回電時，我會再和他談細節。

A Just a minute.
Could you talk slower so I can write down the message for Mr. Gates please?

5

B Yes, let me repeat that.

> **A** 請等一下。
> 你能不能講慢一點，這樣我才能幫蓋茲先生把整個留言記下來？
>
> **B** 好的，我會重講一次。

A Could you talk slower?
I didn't understand what you were asking.

6

B Yes. I would be happy to repeat that.

> **A** 你可以講慢一點嗎？
> 我不太明白你的問題。
>
> **B** 好的，沒問題，我可以再重複一次。

情境對話

A Is Osha there?
奧莎在嗎？

B Sorry. She is out of town and won't be back for two weeks.
抱歉，她出城去了，要兩個星期才會回來。

Can I take a message?
要留言嗎？

A Yes. Tell her that Mona, Julie, Nicole, and Claire are planning to meet at Aaron's house on the twenty-third, but Bryan and Tina cannot come.
好的，請告訴她：「夢娜、茱莉、妮可和克萊兒計畫 23 號要到艾倫家碰面，但布萊恩和提娜無法去。」

B Wait. Could you talk slower?
等一下，你可以說慢一點嗎？

I don't think I got that right.
我聽不太清楚。

A Sure. Bryan and Tina cannot come to Aaron's.
沒問題，布萊恩和提娜沒法去艾倫家。
The rest of us can.
但其他人都沒問題。

B Okay. Thanks and I will get it to her when she comes back.
好的，謝謝，她回來時。我會轉達你的留言。

notes

Chapter **2**

休閒娛樂

現代人愈來愈重視「休閒娛樂」了，如何讓一口好英語幫助你達到盡情玩樂的目的呢？往下看就知道。

Unit

7

MP3-8

Going to the Movies
看電影

情境對話

A Could you tell me where to buy tickets for "Men in Black"?

你能否告訴我哪裡可以買到「星際戰警」的電影票？

B You can get your tickets here, but I am afraid we are all sold out tonight.

這裡就可以買票，但今晚的票恐怕都賣完了。

Would you like to see another movie?

你要不要看別的電影？

A No, thank you.

不用了，謝謝。

B Would you like to purchase tickets for a different showing of "Men in Black"?

你想要買「星際戰警」其他場次的票嗎？

A Is that possible?

可以嗎？

B Sure. You can buy your tickets in advance anytime.

當然，你任何時間都可以預先購票。

例句隨身包

❶ Can you tell me where this movie is showing?

你能否告訴我哪裡有上映這部電影？

❷ Can I buy tickets in advance?

我可以買預售票嗎？

❸ Could you give me two adult tickets for the 10:15 showing of "True Lies"?

我能不能買兩張 10 點 15 分「魔鬼大帝真實謊言」的成人票？

❹ Can I please have two tickets to the seven o'clock showing of "Beauty and the Beast"?

我能否買兩張七點鐘「美女與野獸」的票？

❺ I need four student tickets, please.

我要買四張學生票。

❻ I need two children's and one adult ticket for Friday's showing of "Batman".

我需要買星期五上映的「蝙蝠俠」的票,兩張小孩、一張成人票。

❼ Where is the bathroom?

廁所在哪裡?

❽ Where is the concession stand?

零食攤在哪裡?

❾ May I have a large popcorn and two medium soft drinks, please?

我想買一份大的爆米花和兩杯中杯冷飲。

Unit

8

MP3-9

Going to a Concert
去聽演唱會

情境對話

A I need to buy two extra tickets.
我要再多買兩張票。

Do you have any available?
還有票嗎？

B Yes. They are not far from your original seats either.
有的，而且離你原先購買的位置不太遠。

Are these okay?
這樣的位置可以嗎？

A Yes. Thank you.
可以，謝謝。

41

And can you tell me what exit to take off the highway?

還有，你能否告訴我要在高速公路的哪一個出口下來？

B Sure. Second Street.

沒問題，二街的出口。

And leave early because the traffic will be bad.

你要早點出門，因為交通會很擁擠。

A Will I be able to park my car?

有地方可以停車嗎？

B Yes. There is a parking fee, though.

有的，但是要收費。

Let me give you a number to call if you have any other questions.

我再告訴你另一個電話號碼，如果你有問題的話，可以打去問。

例句隨身包

❶ Can you please tell me where I can buy Rolling Stones tickets?
能否告訴我，哪裡可以買到滾石演唱會的票？

❷ I would like to buy two front row tickets, please.
我想要買兩張前排的票。

❸ Is this the line for the concert tickets?
這是買演唱會票的隊伍嗎？

❹ Can I buy concert tickets over the phone?
我可以用電話購買演唱會的票嗎？

❺ I need to buy tickets.
我要買票。

Do you know where else I can get tickets?
你知道還有其他售票的地方嗎？

❻ I'm trying to win tickets from the radio station.

我試著要贏得電台所提供的演唱會門票。

❼ I have already bought the tickets, but can you tell me where to go to pick them up?

我票已經買了，但你能否告訴我要去哪裡拿票？

❽ They charge for parking, so where should we meet to carpool to the concert?

停車要收費，所以我們要先在哪裡會面，再共乘一輛車過去呢？

Chapter **3**

購物

現代人愈來愈重視「休閒娛樂」了，如何讓一口好英語幫助你達到盡情玩樂的目的呢？往下看就知道。

Unit

9

MP3-10

At the Supermarket
在超市

示範對話

A Would you like plastic or paper?

B I would like plastic bags for my groceries, please.

A 你要塑膠袋還是紙袋？
B 我買的東西要用塑膠袋裝。

情境對話

A Hello. How are you this morning?
嗨，你今天早上好嗎？

B Fine, thanks.
很好，謝謝。

46

How are you?
你呢？

A Good, thanks.
還不錯，謝謝。

Is this going to be all for you?
你就買這些嗎？

B Yes, thank you.
是的，謝謝。

Do you take checks here?
你們收支票嗎？

A Yes. We just need your driver's license number.
可以，只需要知道你的駕照號碼。

B Sure. Let me get it out right now.
沒問題，我馬上拿給你。

例句隨身包

❶ Excuse me, sir, but is this lettuce on sale?
先生，抱歉，這個萵苣有特價嗎？

❷ What aisle is the milk in?
牛奶在第幾行？

❸ What is the difference between these two brands of apples?
這兩種品牌的蘋果有何不同？

❹ Can you help me find the ice cream aisle?
你可不可以幫我找一下冰淇淋放在哪一行？

❺ Can I fill my prescription at this grocery store?
這家商店有沒有賣處方藥？

❻ Is this lane open?
這個結帳出口是否開放？

❼ How would you like to pay for this□cash, check, or credit card?
你要如何付款：現金、支票或信用卡？

Unit

10

MP3-11

Buying Appliances
買電器用品

情境對話

A Excuse me, sir. I need a new microwave.
先生，抱歉，我要買一台新的微波爐。

Can you help me find one?
能不能幫我推薦一台？

B Sure. Are you looking for a specific brand?
當然，你想買某一品牌嗎？

A No. I just want something small.
沒有，我只想要買一台小的。

I don't have enough room for a big microwave.
我沒有空間可以放置一台大的微波爐。

B Okay. Well, there are a lot of good clearance items if you are interested.

好的，如果你有興趣的話，我們有許多大清倉的貨品。

A They aren't used, are they?

它們不是二手貨吧？

B No. Some have been out on the floor as displays or are discontinued brands.

不是，有些是展示品，另一些則是停止生產的品牌。

例句隨身包

❶ Can you tell me where the toasters are?

你能否告訴我烤麵包機放在哪裡？

❷ I am interested in buying a washer and dryer.

我想要買洗衣機和烘乾機。

Can you show me some of your best ones?

你可以介紹一下你們最好的一些品牌嗎？

❸ I like this blender. Do you know if it comes in black?

我喜歡這個果汁機，你知不知道這個樣式有沒有黑色的？

❹ I am looking for a special kind of vacuum. Can you help me?

我正在找一種特別的吸塵器，你可以幫我嗎？

❺ I need a microwave much larger than this. Do you have any?

我需要比這個更大的微波爐，你們有這樣的樣式嗎？

❻ Is this dishwasher on sale?

這個洗碗機有特價嗎？

❼ I am interested in buying a dishwasher.

我想買一台洗碗機。

Can you explain to me your payment plans?

你能否解釋一下你們的付款計畫？

❽ Where would the coffeemakers be?

哪裡可以找到咖啡機？

Buying Household Items
買家用品

情境對話

A I would like to buy more of these window shades.
我想要再買一些這種窗簾。

Do you have any in the back?
你們後面倉庫裡還有沒有？

B I am not sure.
我不確定。

Let me look.
讓我查一下。

A I don't care what color they are.
我不太在乎顏色。

I just want the ones on sale.
我只想要買特價品。

B If that is a sale item, then that is all we are going to have.

如果那一個是特價品，那目前架子上的就是我們有的了。

A Will you get anymore in?

你們還會再進貨嗎？

I have six windows and only four shades.

我有六扇窗戶，但只有四個窗簾。

B No, but we do have some others that have about the same design right here.

不會了，但我們這邊還有一些其他類似的花樣。

Do you like these?

你喜歡這些樣式嗎？

例句隨身包

❶ I need to buy some cookie sheets.

我需要買一些烤餅乾盤。

Where are they?

它們放在哪裡？

❷ Where might we find wooden spoons?

哪裡可以找到木製湯匙？

❸ Why are these towels more expensive than those?

為什麼這些毛巾比那些貴？

❹ I think I would like a blue rug.

我想買一條藍色地毯。

Do you have any on sale?

有沒有特價品？

❹ I need to buy bowls and plates.

我要買一些碗盤。

❻ Can I buy just one of these cups, or do you have to buy the whole set?

我可以單買一個這種茶杯嗎，還是必須買一整套？

❼ I need to buy a trash can this size, but can I buy it in blue?

我需要買這種大小的垃圾桶，但我想要買藍色的？

❽ I am looking for pillows that match this fabric.

我正在找能夠和這種布料搭配的枕頭。

Do you have any in stock?

你們有庫存嗎？

Unit

12

MP3-13

Buying Clothing
買衣服

情境對話

A I am looking for a shirt to match these pants.
我正在找能夠搭配這條褲子的襯衫。

Do you have anything that would work?
你這裡有可以搭配的樣式嗎？

B Sure. Are you looking for something casual or dressy?
當然，你要找的是比較適合日常生活、還是比較正式一點的樣式呢？

A Just something plain and casual.
樣式不要太花俏，輕鬆一點就好。

B What size do you need?
你穿幾號呢？

A Small, please.
小號就可以了。

B How about these?
這些怎麼樣？

Try them on and let me know if they work.
試一下吧，讓我知道他們是否合適？

例句隨身包

❶ I would like to try on this shirt.
我想要試穿這件襯衫。

Can you tell me where the dressing room is?
你能否告訴我試衣間在哪裡？

❷ I like this skirt, but do you have it in my size?
我喜歡這件襯衫，但有我的尺寸嗎？

❸ Does this blouse come in any color but white?
這件上衣除了白色，還有沒有其他顏色？

❹ Do you carry these pants in just white?
這件褲子你們有沒有純白色的？

❺ Is this dress marked down?
這件洋裝有降價嗎？

❻ I bought this dress last week, but can I exchange it for that long-sleeved dress?
我上週買了這件洋裝，可不可以換那件長袖洋裝？

❼ I like these jeans, but can I try them in another size?
我喜歡這件牛仔褲，可不可以試穿別個尺寸？

❽ I don't want these dresses anymore.
我不想要這些洋裝。
Can I get a refund?
我可以退錢嗎？

❾ I want to buy this dress, but I won't have any money for another two weeks.
我想要買這件洋裝，但我還要再等兩週才會有錢。
Can I put it on lay away and just get it later?
你可以先幫我保留這件，我過些時候再過來買？

Unit

13

MP3-14

Buying Shoes
買鞋子

情境對話

A I think I am ready to check out now.
我想我可以結帳了。

B Okay. Are you buying both pairs of shoes?
好的,你兩雙鞋子都要買嗎?

A No, just the white dress shoes.
沒有,只有那雙比較正式的白鞋。

The loafers did not fit right.
那雙平底鞋不是很合腳。

B Would you like to try on another pair?
你要不要再試試看另一雙呢?

We have several different styles.
我們有好幾個不同的樣式。

A No, thanks.　I will just take this pair.

謝謝，不用了，我就買這雙吧。

B How would you like to pay for this—cash, check, or credit card?

您要用現金、支票還是信用卡付帳呢？

例句隨身包

❶ Can you tell me where I can return these sandals?

你能否告訴我，我要去哪裡退這雙涼鞋？

❷ Are you having a buy-one-get-one-free sale?

現在是否有買一送一的的特惠？

❸ Could I try on these boots in nine and a half, please?

這雙靴子我可不可以試穿九號半的尺寸？

❹ I like this particular pair of shoes, but do you have them in a smaller size?

我喜歡這雙特別的鞋子，你有沒有小一點的尺寸？

5 Is this pair of loafers on sale?
這雙平底鞋有特價嗎？

And are they made with real leather?
它們是不是真皮製的？

6 I am looking for a pair of sneakers.
我要找一雙布鞋。

Can you help me find one?
能不能幫我介紹一下？

7 How can I tell if the shoes fit properly?
我怎麼知道鞋子合腳呢？

Unit

14

MP3-15

Buying Cosmetics and Perfumes
買化妝品和香水

情境對話

A　I need to buy some blush.
　　我要買一些腮紅。

　　Can you help me find the right color?
　　能不能幫我推薦適合的顏色？

B　Sure. Do you want a powder blush or liquid?
　　當然，妳要粉狀還是液狀？

A　I always use liquid. It stays on longer.
　　我一直都用液狀的，比較持久。

　　I am more concerned about the right color though.
　　我比較在意的是顏色。

B Okay. Why don't you try a few of these and tell me which you like best?

好的，妳試試看這些顏色，告訴我哪一種妳最喜歡？

A I usually wear a pink tone.

我通常都抹粉紅色系。

Does that have a natural look?

這個看起來自不自然？

B I think you might want to go with a darker color.

我認為妳也許應該試試看比較深的顏色。

Let's try this shade instead.

試試看這個顏色吧。

例句隨身包

❶ What is the difference between pressed powder and loose powder?

粉餅和粉盒有何不同？

❷ I need some eye shadow.

我要買一些眼影。

What colors do you have?
你有什麼顏色可以選？

❸ I would like to buy some black eyeliner.
我想要買一些黑色眼線筆。

What is the best brand?
哪一個品牌最好？

❹ Is this lipstick color a warm color or a cool color?
這隻口紅的顏色是暖色系還是冷色系？

❺ Can you tell me where you keep the make-up remover?
你能否告訴我卸妝液放在哪裡？

❻ May I try that perfume?
我可以試試看那個香水嗎？

❼ I would like to buy a bottle of perfume.
我想要買一瓶香水。

What kinds do you carry?
你有哪些品牌？

8 I need lip-gloss. Do you sell that here?
我要買亮脣膏，這裡有賣嗎？

9 Could you help me pick out some perfume for my wife?
你可以幫我選一些香水嗎？我要送給我太太的。

It's for her birthday.
那是要送她的生日禮物。

Chapter 4

外出用餐

所謂民以食為天，學好英語，可
以免於在外「餓肚子」。

15

Ordering Food
點餐

示範對話

A I would like the peppered steak, but could you hold the mushrooms, please?

B Okay. No mushrooms.
How would you like that cooked?

A Medium-well. I'd like a Sprite, too, please.

> **A** 我想要點胡椒牛排，可是請不要加蘑菇。
> **B** 好的，不加蘑菇。
> 你要幾分熟？
> **A** 七分熟，我還要一杯雪碧。

情境對話

A Hello. My name is Dan and I will be your waiter for the evening.

嗨，我叫丹，我是你們今晚的侍者。

B Hello.
嗨。

A What would you like to start off to drink with tonight?
今晚用餐前，要不要先點一些飲料？

B A vanilla shake, please.
我要一杯香草奶昔。

A All right. Would you like to hear our specials for this evening?
好的，您想不想聽聽我們今晚的特餐內容？

B No, thanks. I'll just look at the menu.
不用了，謝謝，我看菜單就好。

例句隨身包

❶ Can you please give me two large value meals with Dr. Pepper?
我要點兩份大超值特餐，外加汽水。

❷ Can we have a large cheese pizza, please?
我們要點一份大的起司披薩？

❸ Instead of green beans with my order, can I have a salad instead?
我點的餐點裡，能不能不要豆子，改成沙拉？

❹ Can I have a cheeseburger without ketchup or mustard?
我要點一個起司漢堡，不加蕃茄醬或芥茉。

❺ Could you repeat our order so that we can make sure we got everything?
你能不能重複我們所點的菜，確定我們都點齊了？

❻ Can you tell me the difference between the two salads on the menu?
能否解釋一下菜單上兩種沙拉有何不同？

Unit

16

MP3-17

Making Payments
付款

示範對話

A Did you enjoy your food, ladies?

B Yes, thank you.
We are ready for our check now.

A 女士們，用餐一切順利嗎？
B 是的，謝謝。
我們可以結帳了。

情境對話

A Thank you for dining with us this evening.
謝謝您今晚到本餐廳用餐。

I hope you enjoyed it and have a nice evening.
希望您用餐愉快，晚安。

69

B Do I pay up front?

我要到前面結帳嗎？

A Yes.

是的。

B Do you accept American Express cards?

你們收不收美國運通卡？

A Sure. Do you want the entire bill on the credit card?

當然，你要用信用卡支付整個帳單嗎？

B Yes.

是的。

例句隨身包

❶ Did you have a good time?

大家吃得愉快嗎？

I think I will leave our waiter four dollars. Is that enough?

我想我會給那位服務生四塊錢小費，這樣夠不夠？

❷ I heard you just double the tax on the receipt to find out about how much the tip would be.
我聽說你只要把帳單上的稅乘以二，就可以知道小費要付多少。

It is like taking fifteen percent of the check.
相當於帳單的 15%。

❸ Can I write a check here?
我可以用支票付帳嗎？

❹ Here is your check.
這是你們的帳單。

I will take care of it whenever you are ready.
什麼時候準備好了，隨時叫我。

❺ What credit cards do you accept?
你們收哪些信用卡？

Unit

17

MP3-18

Fast Food
速食

情境對話

A　Can I take your order?
可以點菜了嗎？

B　Can I have a few minutes, please?
可以再等幾分鐘嗎？

A　Yes. Order when you're ready.
好的，您可以考慮好了再點。

B　I would like a number two combo meal with a vanilla milkshake and one cheeseburger, please.
我要點二號套餐，加上一杯香草奶昔，另外再加一個起士漢堡。

A　Is that going to be all for you today?
還要再加些什麼嗎？

B Yes. And we would like it to go, please.

不用了，這些是要外帶的。

例句隨身包

❶ Can I get a hamburger and medium fries to go, please?

我要外帶一個漢堡和中號薯條。

❷ Do you take cash only?

你們只收現金嗎？

❸ May I have two tacos, please?
We will be eating here.

我們要點兩個玉米餅，內用。

❹ May I have a refill on Dr. Pepper?

我要汽水續杯。

❺ Can you break a fifty-dollar bill?

這張 50 元美鈔你找得開嗎？

❻ What does your combo meal include?

你們的套餐包括哪些東西？

❼ Where are your napkins and straws?

餐巾和吸管在哪裡？

❽ Can I smoke here?

這裡可以吸煙嗎？

Unit

18

MP3-19

Nice Restaurants
好餐廳

情境對話

A How long is the wait for a party of six?
六人座的桌子要等多久？

B It will be about an hour.
大約要一個鐘頭。

What is the name of your party?
您的名字是？

A Fedar. And can we have a table in the smoking section, please?
法德，麻煩一下，我們要吸煙區的座位。

B Sure. We will call as soon as your table is available.
好的，有位子時，我們會廣播你的名字。

A   Thank you. Is the bar open?

謝謝，吧台有開放嗎？

B   Yes. You can wait in the bar or in the lobby.

有的，您可以在吧台或大廳等。

例句隨身包

❶ Can we have a table for five please?

我們要一個五個人的桌子。

❷ May we have a table in the non-smoking section instead?

可不可以換一個在非吸煙區的桌子？

❸ How long is the wait to be seated?

要等多久才能入座？

❹ We need a table for five, but can we wait until everyone in our party is here to sit down?

我們要一個五個人的桌子，但可不可以等人到齊了才入座？

❺ Do you have a salad bar here?
你們這裡有沙拉吧嗎？

❻ Do you take checks here?
這裡收支票嗎？

❼ We are expecting another couple to join us, but may we be seated first, please?
稍後還有兩個人要來，但我們可以先入座嗎？

❽ Do you have low-fat selections on your menu?
你們菜單上有沒有低熱量的餐點？

19

MP3-20

Call for Catering
打電話安排外燴

情境對話

A I need to confirm my order for tomorrow at noon.

我要確認明天中午的訂席。

B Order for Johnston, party of twenty?

強斯頓先生，20 個人。

A Yes, that is correct.

是的，沒錯。

B And the address is 1524 Windcave, right?

地址是風岈街 1524 號，對嗎？

A Yes. Will drinks be provided?

是的，你們會準備飲料嗎？

B Yes, sir. We will take care of everything for you.

有的，所有細節我們都會照顧到。

例句隨身包

❶ Can we choose from a variety of foods?
我們有許多不同的食物可供選擇嗎？

❷ How much would it cost to cater a party of fifty?
準備 50 個人席次的餐飲要多少錢？

❸ Can you deliver at noon tomorrow?
可以明天中午送達嗎？

❹ Can I add to my previous order, please?
我可以追加之前的訂席嗎？

❺ What is included in your catering service?
你們的外燴服務中包含什麼項目？

6 Will it be cheaper for me to pick up the order?

我自己去拿會不會比較便宜？

7 Do you carry a low-fat selection as well?

有沒有準備低熱量的菜色？

8 Will I need to pay in advance?

我需要先付錢嗎？

Chapter 5

保健英語

　　最幸福的人，最幸運的人，一定少不了「健康」。為你的健康把關，快點把「保健英語」學起來吧！

Unit

20

MP3-21

Making an Appointment
預約

情境對話

A I would like to make an appointment for today.
我想預約今天。

B For which doctor?
和哪一位醫生？

A Dr. Hughes.
修伊醫生。

B I am sorry. He is completely booked today.
抱歉，他今天都約滿了。

A What about Dr. Keasler?
肯斯樂醫生可以嗎？

B He has an opening for eleven this morning and one for four-thirty this afternoon.

他今天早上十一點和下午四點半有空。

Does either of those fit your schedule?

這兩個當中有沒有一個比較適合你的時間？

 例句隨身包

❶ My son is sick. Can I make an appointment for today?

我兒子生病了，我可以預約今天嗎？

❷ Is it possible to come in today for a blood test?

今天可以過來做血液檢查嗎？

❸ The doctor told me to come back in two weeks.

醫生要我兩星期內回診。

Do you have an opening for two weeks from Thursday around one?

兩星期後的星期四下午一點有空嗎？

❹ My husband has cut his hand.
我先生切傷了自己的手。

Do I need to go to the emergency room, or can you see him right now?
我需要去掛急診，還是你現在有空可以看看他？

❺ My daughter has a temperature of 101°F.
我女兒發燒到華氏 101 度。

Should she come in today?
是不是應該今天過來看病？

❻ I know Dr. Hartford is on vacation, but can I make an appointment with another doctor for today?
我知道華特醫生正在休假，但我能否預約其他醫生今天的時間？

❼ Is it possible to come in Thursday around two o'clock?
我可以在星期四下午兩點鐘時過來嗎？

❽ Are you closed on Saturdays?
你們星期六休診嗎？

Unit

21

MP3-22

Talking to the Nurse
和護士溝通

A What symptoms have you had?
你有什麼症狀？

B I have been coughing and sneezing, and I have had a fever and headaches for the past few days.
我一直咳嗽、打噴嚏，過去幾天還發燒和頭痛。

A What has been your average temperature?
平均體溫是多少？

B About 100 degrees.
華氏 100 度。

A What has been your normal diet?
通常都吃些什麼東西？

B I haven't felt well enough to eat much.

我不舒服，所以吃不多。

I've mainly been eating soup.

主要都是喝湯。

例句隨身包

❶ Do I take my temperature under my tongue?

我要量口溫嗎？

❷ Can I take my temperature under my arm instead?

可不可以量腋溫？

❸ Lately I have had morning sickness and been feeling faint. Could I be pregnant?

最近我早上都不太舒服，有些暈暈的，有沒有可能是懷孕了呢？

❹ What are the common symptoms of the flu?
流行性感冒的一般症狀為何？

❺ I don't feel very well.
我覺得不太舒服。

Where are the water fountains?
哪裡有飲水機？

❻ Does she have to stay in the waiting room, or can she come with me?
她必須在候診室等，還是可以和我一起進去？

❼ When will the doctor come in to see me?
醫生什麼時候才能見我？

❽ I think I am going to throw up.
我想我快吐了。

Where are the bathrooms?
廁所在哪裡？

22

Talking to a Doctor
和醫生交談

情境對話

A What are your symptoms?
你有什麼症狀？

B I have had headaches, coughing fits, and a sore throat.
我一直會頭疼、咳個不停，還有喉嚨痛。

A Any fever?
有發燒嗎？

B No.
沒有。

A Are you allergic to anything?
有沒有對什麼東西過敏？

B No.

沒有。

❶ Can you refer me to another doctor, please?

你可以介紹我看另一位醫生嗎？

❷ When will I be able to go back to work?

我什麼時候可以回去上班？

❸ Are these tests covered by my insurance?

這些檢驗我的保險會不會給付？

❹ Should I come back for another check up?

我要再回來進行另一次檢查嗎？

❺ I am moving to Paris, Texas.
我要搬到德州巴理市。

Can you refer me to any doctors there?
你可不可以推薦我幾位那裡的醫生？

❻ I haven't been eating right lately.
我最近都吃得不太好。

Is that why I am sick?
我是因為這樣才生病的嗎？

❼ Can you write me a docto's note, please?
你可不可以幫我寫張看病證明？

❽ Is there a number I can call for information in case my son gets sick again?
如果我兒子又再生病，有哪個電話我可以打的？

Unit

23

MP3-24

Asking about a Prescription
開處方

情境對話

A Would you prefer liquid or pills for your prescription?
你比較喜歡喝藥水還是吃藥丸？

B Pills. I don't like the taste of liquid medicine.
吃藥丸，我不喜歡藥水的味道。

A Okay. The instructions will be on the bottle.
好的，服藥指示會貼在瓶子上面。

You shouldn't feel drowsy, but make sure you eat something with this medication.
你應該不會昏昏欲睡，但要確定不要空腹吃藥。

B Do I just take it twice a day?
一天吃兩次藥嗎？

A Yes. It says so on the bottle.
是的，瓶身上的指示是這樣説。

Just get plenty of rest and you should be back to work in a few days.
好好休息，應該幾天後就可以恢復上班。

B Thank you. Is there a number I can call if I have any questions?
謝謝，如果我有疑問的話，可以撥哪個電話？

例句隨身包

❶ How will I know if I have an allergic reaction to the medicine?
我怎麼知道自己是否對某種藥物會過敏？

❷ Will I need a refill?
我需要再重複拿藥嗎？

❸ What kind of side effects does this medicine have?
這個藥有什麼副作用嗎？

❹ Do I take this prescription with food?
這個藥需要配食物一起吃嗎?

❺ Can I go back to work on this medication?
吃這個藥可以上班嗎?

❻ Do I take this medicine in the morning and at night?
我是否早晚要服用這個藥?

❼ What happens if I forget to take my medicine three times a day?
如果我一天三餐沒有照常服藥會怎麼樣?

❽ Do I just apply this medication to the rash?
我是不是直接把這個藥擦在疹子上?

Unit

24

MP3-25

At the Pharmacy
在藥房

情境對話

A　I am here to pick up a prescription for Meyer.
我過來拿處方藥給邁爾。

B　Did your doctor call it in?
你的醫生來過電話了嗎？

A　I believe so.
我想是吧。

B　The pharmacist hasn't filled your prescription.
藥師還沒有把你的藥配好。

It is going to be about ten more minutes.
你還要等個十分鐘。

A Can I pay for my prescription now?
我可以先付錢嗎？

B Yes. We take cash, credit cards, and checks.
可以，我們收取現金、信用卡及支票。

例句隨身包

1 Does my health insurance cover this medication?
我的健保是否給付這個藥？

❷ When will my prescription be available?
我的處方藥什麼時候可以拿？

❸ Where do I go if I need a refill?
如果我要續藥，要到哪裡去呢？

❹ What is the difference between these two prescriptions?
這兩個處方之間有何不同？

❺ Why is this medication not available over the counter?

為什麼這個藥需要處方？

❻ Do I pay for my prescription here?

我的處方藥是在這裡付款嗎？

❼ Whom do I call if I have questions regarding my medication?

如果我碰到關於服藥的問題，要聯絡誰呢？

Unit

25

MP3-26

Talking to a Pharmacist
和藥師談話

情境對話

A I think I am having an allergic reaction to my prescription.

我想我對這個處方藥過敏。

B Why?

為什麼呢？

A The medicine leaves a bad taste in my mouth.

這個藥讓我嘴巴味道很難聞。

B Have you read the information sheet that came with the medication?

你有沒有閱讀這個藥所附的資料？

A Yes.

有。

B It should only last a few days.

這種狀況應該只會持續幾天而已。

Let me give you a number you can call if you have any more questions.

如果你還有其他問題的話，可以打我給你的這個電話。

Don't worry, Mr. Kalny. You should be well again in a few days.

卡尼先生，別擔心，你應該幾天之內就會康復了。

 例句隨身包

❶ What side effects does this medication have?

這個藥有什麼副作用？

❷ How do I know if my son is allergic to this prescription?

我怎麼知道我兒子會不會對這藥方過敏呢？

❸ Should I take all the pills in this bottle?

我應該把這罐子裡的藥丸全部吃完嗎？

4 Can I still drive a car if I take this medicine?

吃了這個藥，我可以開車嗎？

5 Why do I need to take this medicine with food?

為什麼這個藥得配食物服用？

6 Is there any way to prevent this medicine from making me drowsy?

有沒有辦法預防這個藥可能造成的暈眩效果？

7 Why does this medicine leave a bad taste in my mouth?

為什麼這個藥會讓我嘴巴有不好的味道？

8 Will I need another refill?

我需要再續藥嗎？

Unit

26

MP3-27

Looking for Over-the-Counter Drugs
買成藥

情境對話

A Excuse me. Can you tell me where the Excedrin is, please?
抱歉，可不可以告訴我普拿疼放在哪裡？

B Third aisle on the left.
左邊第三行。

A Is that what I take for headaches?
它對頭疼有效嗎？

B Yes. Almost everything you find there should help with headaches.
有的，那一排的藥幾乎都可以治頭疼。

A Do I need maximum strength?
我需要買超級特效的嗎？

B Maximum strength and regular strength are basically the same.

超級特效和普級特效基本上是一樣的。

例句隨身包

❶ Can you tell me what is the best headache medicine I can buy over the counter?

能否告訴我治頭疼最有效、而不用處方箋的藥是什麼？

❷ What is the difference between Advil and Tylenol?

Advil 和 Tylenol 這兩種頭痛藥有什麼不同？

❸ Can you tell me where the children's cough medicine is located?

能否告訴我小孩子的咳嗽藥放在哪裡？

❹ Does it tell me how many gel capsules are in this box?

有沒有提到一盒中有幾個膠囊？

❺ Are there any over-the-counter medications or creams that I can buy for burns?

有沒有任何不用處方箋就可以買的燙傷藥或藥膏？

❻ How many of these can I take within a 24-hour period?

24 小時內，這藥物可以服用幾次？

❼ Do you have chewable medicine for children?

有沒有適合小孩子咀嚼的藥？

❽ What is the difference between the medication the doctor prescribes and this over-the-counter medicine for the flu?

醫生所開的治流行性感冒藥，和一般藥房可以買到的成藥有何不同？

Part 3 Health Consultation 健康諮詢

Unit

27

MP3-28

How to Find a Good Doctor
如何找一個好醫生

情境對話

A I got your name and number from a friend at work.
我從同事那裡拿到你的名字和電話。

She said you were an excellent doctor.
她說你是一位很棒的醫生。

Do you mind if I ask you a few questions?
你介不介意我向你請教幾個問題？

B Not at all. Go right ahead.
不會，您儘管問。

A How long have you been practicing medicine?
你執業多久了？

B Almost ten years.
幾乎十年了。

A Can you give me some background information?
你可以給我一些妳的背景資料嗎？

B I worked at Baylor Medical Center for many years and opened my own practice five years ago.
我以前在貝爾醫學中心服務多年，然後在五年前開了自己的診所。

I have a staff of three other doctors and about ten medical assistants.
我目前有三位醫生和十位醫療助理。

例句隨身包

❶ Excuse me, ma'am.
小姐，請問一下。

Do you have a list of doctors at this clinic?
你有沒有你們診所全部的醫生名冊？

❷ Sally, I am looking for a doctor.
莎莉，我想看醫生。

Do you like yours?
妳建議妳的醫生嗎？

❸ Mr. McAvery, I am new in town and I'm looking for a new doctor.
麥可維爾先生，我剛剛搬到這裡，想找一位新的醫生。

Do you recommend anyone?
你有沒有什麼建議？

❹ I am just calling to get some information on your doctors.
我打電話的原因是想了解一下你們這邊的醫生。

I found your number in the yellow pages.
你們的電話號碼有列在黃頁電話簿中。

❺ Hello. Is this Dr. Kay? A friend of mine referred you to me.

嗨，凱醫生在嗎？我的朋友向我推薦你。

Can you give me some background information about your doctor's office?

你能否給我一些有關你們診所的背景資料？

❻ I am looking for a new doctor, and your name was given to me by my health insurance company.

我在找新的醫生，我的保險公司把你的名字給了我。

Can you answer a few of my questions?

能否請你回答我一些問題？

❼ I saw your ad in the newspaper.

我看到你們在報紙上的廣告。

Can you give me some more information about your clinic?

能否提供我一些有關你們診所的資料？

Unit

28

MP3-29

Most Frequent Symptoms
最常見的症狀

情境對話

A　What seems to be the problem?
　　有什麼不舒服的地方？

B　My head hurts, it is hard to breathe, and my nose is running all the time.
　　我頭痛，呼吸困難，一直流鼻水。

A　Have you been coughing much?
　　有沒有咳嗽的很厲害？

B　Yes. It hurts to cough, though.
　　有，咳嗽時候會痛。

A　Is your temperature high?
　　有沒有發燒？

B Not all the time.
斷斷續續。

❶ My throat is dry and it hurts.
我喉嚨很乾、很痛。

I think I have a sore throat.
我想應該是喉嚨發炎吧。

❷ My arms, back, neck, and stomach itch. Do I have a rash?
我的手臂、脖子和腹部都會癢。這是起疹子嗎？

❸ I think I have allergies.
我想我過敏了。

❹ She feels very hot. Maybe she has a fever.
她覺得很熱，也許發燒了。

❹ The baby won't stop crying and she keeps grabbing her ear.
寶寶一直哭個不停，一直抓耳朵。

She may have an ear infection.
可能是耳朵發炎了。

❻ My stomach hurts. I think I have cramps.
我胃痛，我想是胃痙攣。

❼ She is at the hospital. The doctors said she has pneumonia.
她住院了，醫生說她感染肺炎。

❽ What do I take to get rid of a headache?
要吃什麼藥才能使頭痛停止？

Unit

29

MP3-30

Health Insurance
健康保險

情境對話

A Hello.
嗨。

B My name is Mrs. Hanover, and I need some information about your health insurance coverage.
我的名字是海歐爾太太，我想要一些有關保險給付項目的資料。

A Okay. We would be happy to mail you out something today.
好的，我們很樂意寄給妳這方面的資料，今天就會寄出。

B Great. My address is 542 Parker Place. That is in Plano.
太好了，我的地址是布南諾市帕克街 542 號。

I would like to change health insurance for my entire family.

我想幫所有家人挑另一個健保計畫。

A We will send you a packet of information.

我們會寄給妳一疊資料。

B When can I expect the information?

大概什麼時候會收到呢？

例句隨身包

❶ How can I find out more about your health insurance plan?

我要如何知道更多有關你們健康保險的給付內容？

❷ Can you send me information by mail?

你可以郵寄一些資料給我嗎？

❸ Can I go to your offices to find out about your insurance plans?

我可以過去拜訪你們，索取一些有關保險計畫的資料嗎？

❹ Will you send someone by my house to explain your insurance plan?

你可以派人過來我們這裡，解釋一下你們的保險計畫內容嗎？

❹ Can we discuss over the phone the insurance options?

我們能否在電話上談一下健康保險的種類有哪些？

❻ Can your company fax me the information?

你們公司可以傳真一些資料給我嗎？

❼ What are the price range of the different policies?

不同的保險的價格範圍大概是多少？

❽ What is included in the different plans?

不同的保險計畫中有何不同內容？

Unit

30

MP3-31

Asking about Insurance Premiums
詢問保費

A Miller's Health Insurance. Can I help you?
米勒健保，有什麼可以為你效勞的嗎？

B I would like some information about your premiums.
我想要索取一些有關你們保費的資料。

A How can I help you?
你想知道哪些資料呢？

B I am planning to move my family to your insurance plan but would like to know how the payment plan works.
我想要把家人的保險計畫換到你們公司，可是我想先知道你們的保費支付方式如何。

113

A We bill you at the beginning of each month.
我們會在每個月初寄帳單給你。

B Is it cheaper to pay for the whole year at once?
一次支付一年的保費是否比較便宜？

A You have the option of paying the full bill, but the price remains the same.
您可以一次付清，但保費沒有差異。

例句隨身包

❶ Can I pay for the insurance yearly?
我可以採年付費的方式嗎？

❷ Do you accept monthly payments?
你們接受月付費的方式嗎？

❸ Can you tell me how am I billed?
你可以告訴我你們會如何收費嗎？

❹ Is it possible to take payments directly out of my checking account?
你們可以直接從我的支票帳戶中扣保費嗎？

❺ Should I expect payment to increase or decrease?

保費有可能調漲或降低嗎？

❻ What is the difference in price between individual coverage and family?

個人保險和家庭保險價格有何不同？

❼ Am I required to sign a contract?

我必須要簽合約嗎？

❽ Can I change my policy?

我可以改變保單內容嗎？

Unit

31

MP3-32

Health Insurance Coverage
健康保險範圍

情境對話

A Excuse me. I have a few questions about my new insurance policy.

抱歉，關於我的新保單，我有幾個問題。

B How can I help you?

您儘管問。

A I would like to know how I choose my doctor.

我想知道我要如何選擇醫生。

B You have probably received a packet of information including all the doctors that are covered in your insurance plan.

你可能已經收到一整疊的資料，其中有加入保險計畫的所有醫生名字。

If you visit a doctor on that list, your insurance covers the cost.

如果你去看的醫生，他的名字在名單中，保險公司就會負擔看診的費用。

A What happens if I choose a doctor outside of the list?

如果我選的醫生不在名單上，情況會怎樣呢？

B Then your insurance will not cover the cost.

那你的保險就不會支付看診費用。

The list is full of very experienced doctors.

這個名單中的醫生經驗都很豐富。

I don't think you will have a problem finding a doctor that is right for you.

我想找一位適合您的醫生，應該不是很困難。

例句隨身包

❶ Does my health insurance include doctor's visits?

我的保險計畫有包含醫生看診費用嗎？

❷ Are prescription drugs covered in the policy?

保單是否給付處方藥？

❸ Can I choose my hospital?

我可以選擇醫院嗎？

❹ How does the insurance cover emergencies?

保險對急診的給付內容如何？

❺ How does my insurance cover preexisting illnesses?

我的保險對於入保之前就有的疾病，有什麼樣的給付？

❻ How long will my insurance cover a hospital stay?

我的保險能夠給付多久的住院期間？

❼ Do I choose my own doctor?

我可以選擇自己的醫生嗎？

❽ Are all tests ordered by my doctor covered?

保險會給付所有我醫生指定的檢驗嗎？

Unit

32

MP3-33

Deductibles and Co-payment
保險扣除額和自付額

A How does your insurance plan handle prescriptions?
你的保險計畫對處方藥如何處理？

B I pay the full cost of the first prescription but only pay twenty dollars for every prescription that follows.
我得支付第一次處方藥的全額，但之後每次只付 20 元。

A Does that apply to your children as well?
這也適用於你的小孩嗎？

B Yes. We are all covered.
是的，我們都有保險。

A Well, my health insurance is covered through my workplace, but I hear there are better plans elsewhere.
我的保險是由公司支付的，但我聽說別處還有更好的保險計畫。

B Maybe you should look into mine.
也許你應該看看我的保險計畫。

例句隨身包

❶ Does this insurance have deductibles?
這個保險有保險扣除額嗎？

❷ How much is the deductible?
保險扣除額是多少？

❸ What is not considered a deductible?
什麼不算保險扣除額？

❹ Are prescription payments considered a deductible?
處方藥的支付算不算是保險扣除額？

❺ What is considered co-payment in your insurance plan?
你的保險計畫中，什麼才算是自付額？

❻ What is the co-payment policy for a doctor's visit?
看醫生的自付額有何相關規定？

❼ Is it the same for hospital stays?
也可適用於住院費用嗎？

❽ Is there a co-payment for emergencies?
急診有自付額嗎？

33

Medical Expense Reimbursement
醫療費用理賠

MP3-34

情境對話

A Can you tell me what I need to be reimbursed?
你能否告訴我要怎麼做，才能理賠？

B You need all of your receipts.
你需要保留所有收據。

A Do I need a special form to get reimbursed?
我需要填特殊的表格，才能申請理賠嗎？

B No. Just mail your receipts to the insurance company.
不用，只要把收據寄給你的保險公司就可以了。

A When can I expect the reimbursement?
大概多久可以收到理賠呢？

B At the end of the month.
月底。

例句隨身包

1　How do I get reimbursed for medical expenses?
　　我要如何才能申請醫療費用的理賠？

❷ What qualifies for reimbursement?
　　什麼項目才能符合費用理賠規定？

❸ Will I be reimbursed for this?
　　這個我之後可以申請費用理賠嗎？

❹ Do I need the doctor's signature?
　　我需要索取醫生的簽名嗎？

❺ Do I need to fill out a special form?
　　我需要填特殊表格嗎？

❻ Are my children covered under reimbursement?
　　我小孩的醫療費用也會被理賠嗎？

❼ Who do I contact for reimbursement?
　　我要聯絡什麼人才能申請費用理賠呢？

❽ How long will I wait to be reimbursed?
　　要等多久才會被理賠呢？

notes

Chapter 6

定居落腳

孔子說：「三十而立」，指的是一個人在各方面都能安然立足。你有租房子的經驗嗎？想有效地找到理想的居所嗎？請看「租屋英語」。

Unit 34

MP3-35

Renting an Apartment
租公寓

情境對話

A I'm interested in renting an apartment.
我想要租一個公寓。

B Okay. What size?
好的,大小是?

A Either a one-bedroom or two-bedroom.
單臥室或雙臥室公寓都行。

What are the differences in the square footage and in the amount of rent per month?
室內大小和每月房租方面有何不同?

B The one-bedroom apartment ranges from 698-788 square feet, and the two-bedroom is 897-1,186 square feet depending on the bedroom/

126

bathroom floor plans.

單臥室公寓的大小大約是 698 ~ 788 平方英尺，雙臥室的大小大約是 897~ 1,186 平方英尺，不同處在於臥室和浴室的大小設計。

Rent starts at $480.

租金最便宜的是 480 元。

A Does that amount include water or electricity?

這個房租是否包含水費或電費？

B Rent includes water but not electricity or cable. Those are extra.

房租包含水費，但不包含電費或有線電視費用，那些都算額外費用。

Let's go look at one of the apartments, and I can show you the pool and tennis courts.

一起去看看其中一間吧，還可以讓你看看游泳池和網球場。

❶ Do you offer three-or four-bedroom apartments?
你們有三房或四房的公寓嗎？

❷ How much is the rent per month?
每月的房租是多少？

❸ What is the difference in the amount of rent between the one-bedroom and the two-bedroom apartments?
單臥室和雙臥室公寓的房租差多少？

❹ Does the rent include water and electricity or are those extra?
房租包含水費和電費嗎，還是它們都是額外的費用？

❺ Are there a washer and dryer?
公寓裡有洗衣機和烘衣機嗎？

Or is there a laundry facility close by?
還是附近有洗衣店？

❻ Is there a pool or a tennis court?
有游泳池或網球場嗎？

❼ How many square feet is the two-bedroom?
一個雙臥室公寓有多大？

❽ How accessible is the parking, and is there a security gate?
停車方便嗎，有沒有警衛大門？

❾ Is there a pet deposit required?
飼養寵物的話，需要繳交保證金嗎？

Dark clouds become heaven's flowers
when kissed by light.

-Rabindranath Tagore

只因陽光的一吻，　雲變成天堂之花。

—泰戈爾

Unit

35

MP3-36

Renting a House
租房子

情境對話

A Hello. I'm calling about the house.
嗨，我想詢問你們要出租的房子。

How many bedrooms does it have?
它有幾間臥室？

B There are three bedrooms and two bathrooms.
三間臥室和兩間浴室。

A How much is the rent, and is there a deposit?
租金多少，需不需要付保證金？

B It's $900 a month with first and last month rent up front.
每月月租 900 元，要先繳付第一個月和最後一個月的租金。

A Can I come by and look at the place tomorrow?
我明天可以過來看看房子嗎？

B Of course.
當然。

 例句隨身包

❶ How many bedrooms are in the house?
房子有幾間臥室？

❷ How many bathrooms are in the house?
房子有幾間浴室？

❸ Is there a garage?
有車庫嗎？

❹ What school district is the house in, and is there a school nearby?
這個房子屬於哪個學區管轄，附近有沒有學校？

❹ Is the rent monthly and does it include utilities?

這房租是月繳的嗎？有沒有涵蓋水電費用？

❻ Do you require a deposit? How much is it?

你是否有要求保證金？金額多少？

❼ Do you allow animals?

你准許房客養動物嗎？

❽ How large is the backyard?

後院有多大？

❾ How are the neighbors?

鄰居如何？

❿ How many square feet is the house?

房子有多少平方英尺？

Unit

36

MP3-37

Buying a House
買房子

情境對話

A Hello. I'd like to make an appointment with a real estate agent.

嗨,我想要和房地產仲介約個時間。

I'm looking to buy a house.

我想要買房子。

B All right. What day would you like?

好的,你想要約哪一天?

A Next Wednesday would be good.

下星期三。

B Would 3:00 Wednesday afternoon be okay?

星期三下午三點可以嗎?

A Yes. Now could you tell me exactly where you are located?

可以，現在請你告訴我你們的詳細位置。

B Sure, I can give you directions.

好的，我會給你路線指示。

Where will you be coming from?

你要從哪裡過來呢？

❶ I'm looking for a real estate agent.

我要找一個房地產仲介。

❷ Could you recommend me a real estate agent?

你可以推薦我一位房地產仲介嗎？

I'm looking to buy a house.

我想要買房子。

❸ Where are your offices located?

你的辦公室位於哪裡？

❹ What are your hours and when can I come by?

你幾點上班，我什麼時候可以過來？

❺ Can I make an appointment for next week?

我可以預約下週的時間嗎？

❻ Where exactly is your office located?

你們公司確實的位置在哪裡？

Taking a Look at the House
看房子

情境對話

B As you can see, the house has big, open rooms with plenty of space; even the closets are huge.
你可以看到，這個房子空間很大，就連衣櫥都很大。

A Is that the hallway to the garage?
那是通往車庫的走道嗎？

B Yes. This door leads to the garage, which also has a door leading into the backyard.
是的，這扇門通往車庫，那裡還有一扇門通往後院。

A That window is cracked.
那扇窗戶破了。

Will that be repaired?
屋主會修好嗎？

B I can ask the owners about that.
我可以問問看屋主。

A Thank you. Now about the price...
謝謝，現在想請教一下價格……。

例句隨身包

❶ We have to meet the agent at 3:00 on Wednesday to preview the house.
我們週三下午三點要和仲介碰面，去看看房子。

❷ Is the house near a school?
那房子靠近學校嗎？

❸ What is the crime rate?
犯罪率如何？

❹ It looks like the roof needs repairs.
看起來屋頂需要整修。

❺ How old is the water heater?
熱水器有多舊了？

❻ How old is the air conditioning unit?
冷氣機有多舊了？

❼ When was the house built?
房子是什麼時候建造的？

❽ There is a broken step on the porch. Will that be fixed?
前廊的階梯有一個壞了，屋主會修好嗎？

❿ How big is the house?
房子有多大？

⓫ How big is the backyard?
後院有多大？

Unit

38

MP3-39

Negotiating the Price
議價

A That price seems a little high.
這個價格似乎有點高。

B It is the same amount the other houses in the area are going for.
這個價格和這區其他房子的出售價格差不多。

It's actually quite reasonable.
實際上還蠻合理的。

A But does that price include repairs?
但這個價格包含了修理費用嗎？

B Yes. They will fix the window, patch the roof, and take care of the broken front step.
是的，屋主會修好窗戶、屋頂和前廊的階梯。

A All right, but I'd like to put in a lower bid.
好的，但我想先出一個低一點的價格。

When can we write up the contract?
我們什麼時候可以擬好合約？

B I'll call you tomorrow about it.
我明天會打電話給你。

例句隨身包

❶ That price seems pretty high.
這價格似乎有些高。

❷ What is the range of the prices of the other homes in the area?
這個地區中，其他房子的價格範圍為何？

❸ The house down the street was sold for $200,000.00 just last week.
街底的那個房子上週才以二十萬美元賣出。

❹ Does the price include repairs?
這個價格包含修理費用嗎?

❺ When can we write up the contract?
我們什麼時候可以擬好合約?

❻ I'd like to offer $180,000.00 for the house.
我想要出價十八萬美元。

Applying for a Loan
申請貸款

A　Bank United. How can I direct your call?
聯合銀行，請問要找哪位？

B　Loan Department, please.
請接貸款部門。

A　Okay. How can I help you?
好的，有什麼可以為你效勞的嗎？

B　I'd like to come in and apply for a loan.
我想要過來申請貸款。

Will I need to bring any papers or information?
我需要帶任何文件或資料嗎？

A You will need proof of employment, a social security card, valid ID, and a completed application.

你需有工作證明、社會安全卡、有效身分證明及填好的申請表。

B Do I need to make an appointment with a loan officer, or can I just walk in?

我需要和貸款人員先預約嗎，還是我可以直接過來？

A I can make an appointment for you. One minute, please.

我可以幫你預約，請等一下。

例句隨身包

❶ I'd like to know where I need to go to apply for a loan, please.

我想請問要到哪裡申請貸款？

❷ Do I need to fill out all these papers?

我需要填這些文件嗎？

❸ Will I need to bring any other information?

我需要攜帶其他資料嗎？

❹ Do I need proof of employment?
我需要帶工作證明嗎？

What kind of proof do you need?
你們要求哪一種證明呢？

❺ Where are the applications?
申請文件呢？

❻ Do I need an ID?
我需要帶身分證明嗎？

Unit

40

MP3-41

Seeing a Loan Officer
與貸款人員見面

情境對話

B Hello. I have a 3:00 appointment with you, Mr. Smith.

嗨,史密斯先生,我和你三點有約。

A Great. Have a seat.

很好,請坐。

Do you have a completed application, valid form of ID, and proof of employment?

你有填好的申請表、有效身分證明和工作證明嗎?

B Yes, I brought them with me.

是的,我把它們帶來了。

A I'll just go make a copy of these for our files and start the credit check.

我先把這些文件影印一份留底,再開始調查您的信用。

B Okay. How long will that take?

好的，這大概要多久的時間？

A We should have the results in two days.

我們大約兩天內就可以有結果。

例句隨身包

❶ I have a 3:00 appointment with Mr. Smith.

我和史密斯先生三點有約。

Where do I need to go?

我該往應該哪裡走？

❷ I brought proof of employment, ID, and a completed application. What else do I need?

我帶來了工作證明、身分證明和填好的申請表，還需要什麼資料嗎？

❸ I don't understand what this form is for.
我不了解這個表格是做什麼的。

Can you explain it again?
能否再解釋一次？

❹ Do I need to sign here?
我應該在這邊簽名嗎？

What am I signing?
我簽的是什麼文件？

❺ Will there be a credit check?
要進行信用調查嗎？

How long will it take?
需費時多久？

❻ Based on my credit history and salary, how much of a loan will I qualify for?
基於我的信用歷史與薪資，我可以申請多少貸款額呢？

❼ How long before I will be approved for a loan?
我要等多久才能拿到貸款？

Asking about Mortgage Rates
詢問關於抵押貸款率

情境對話

A I heard there are different types of mortgage rates based on different types of loans.
我聽說不同貸款，抵押貸款的利率也不同。

Is that true?
是真的嗎？

B Yes. Here is a pamphlet that explains the different kinds of loans our bank offers.
是的，這個小手冊會解釋我們銀行提供的不同貸款。

A What is the highest mortgage rate?
抵押貸款利率最高是多少？

B That depends on the type of loan.
要看是哪一種貸款。

A Okay. What about a FHA loan?

好的，那 FHA 貸款呢？

B If you qualify, the FHA loan has a 7.5% mortgage rate.

如果你資格符合的話，FHA 貸款的利率是 7.5%。

 例句隨身包

❶ I heard there are different types of mortgage rates based on different types of loans but I am not sure I understand.

我聽說不同貸款有不同的貸款利率，我不太了解這是什麼意思。

Can you explain that to me?

可否解釋給我聽？

❷ What kind of loans do I qualify for, and what are their mortgage rates?

我的資格符合什麼樣的貸款，貸款利率又是多少呢？

❸ Do mortgage options depend on the type of loan?

抵押貸款的選擇是否要視貸款類型而定？

❹ What about a FHA loan?

那 FHA 貸款的利率呢？

❺ What are my mortgage options?

我有哪些抵押貸款選擇？

Unit

42

MP3-43

Application was rejected
申請被拒

情境對話

A I got a letter in the mail about my loan application.
我收到關於貸款申請的回函。

Do I need to talk to you about it, Mr. Smith?
史密斯先生，我需要和你談談嗎？

B Yes.
好的。

A What are my options?
我現在有什麼選擇呢？

B The problem was with the credit check.
你的問題出在信用調查。

If you can get that cleared up, you can reapply.
如果你可以解決那個問題，就可以再次提出申請。

A　How do I go about doing that?
我要如何解決信用調查的問題呢？

B　At the bottom of the letter, there should be a number you can call to ask about it.
信的最下方應該有一個電話號碼，你可以打電話去問問看。

例句隨身包

❶ I got a letter in the mail about my loan application.
我收到關於貸款申請的回函。

Who do I need to talk to about it?
我應該和誰談談呢？

❷ What are my options for reapplying?
我重新申請有哪些選擇？

❸ Do I have any options?
我還有其他選擇嗎？

❹ Can I try a different bank?
我可以試試別家銀行嗎？

❺ Is there more information that is needed to reapply?
若要重新申請，是否需要更多的資料？

❻ Is there someone else I can talk to?
我可以找誰請教一下？

❼ What can I do to fix my credit?
我要怎麼改善信用這方面的問題？

Home Improvement
家庭修理

情境對話

A I'm looking for someone to paint my house.
我想找人幫我油漆房子。

Do you charge for estimates?
你們估價要收費嗎？

B No. Do you need the inside or the outside painted?
不用，你需要油漆房子裡面還是外面？

A I'd like to get an estimate for the outside and an estimate for my staircase inside.
我想要房子外觀和裡面樓梯部分油漆的估價。

When could you send someone by?
你什麼時候可以派人過來？

B I can send someone over around noon tomorrow.
我明天中午可以派人過去。

A That will be great.
太好了。

B Okay. Just let me get some information from you.
好的，我只需要您的一些資料。

例句隨身包

❶ I'm looking for a roof repairman.
我正在找修屋頂的人。

Can you come to make an estimate for repairs?
你可以過來估個價嗎？

❷ Can you recommend someone to fix my TV?
你可以推薦人來幫我修電視嗎？

❸ How much do you charge to fix
refrigerators?
修理冰箱要多少錢？

❹ My bathtub drain is clogged.
我浴缸的排水孔堵住了。

When can you send someone over to look
at it?
你什麼時候可以派人過來看看？

❺ How much do you charge per hour?
你一小時收費多少錢？

❻ Do you charge for estimates?
估價要收費嗎？

❼ When can your repairman come by?
你的修理人員什麼時候會過來？

❽ I need to have my house painted.
我房子需要油漆。

How much do you charge?
你的費用怎麼算？

Chapter **7**

學校生活

無論是大人或小孩,想繼續在國外進修或受教育,要如何詢問學校的相關課程呢?

Asking for ESL Classes

詢問是否有 ESL
（學習英文為第二語言）的課程

情境對話

A Do you offer ESL classes at this community college?

請問你們的社區大學有沒有 ESL 課程？

B We do. Are you already registered?

有的，你已經註冊了嗎？

A Yes.

是的。

B Okay. You need to go to the building across the walkway to sign up.

好的，你需要到走道對面的大樓去選課。

The classes are offered through the multicultural program.

該課程是由多文化教程所提供的。

They will help you there.
他們會給你協助。

A Do I need to take anything with me to sign up for ESL classes?
我需要帶什麼東西去選 ESL 的課嗎?

B No. They should have everything in the computer system already.
不用,他們要的資料應該都在電腦系統裡了。

例句隨身包

❶ Are ESL classes offered here?
這裡有沒有 ESL 的課程?

❷ Do you have ESL classes in grade schools and high schools?
你們小學和中學有沒有 ESL 的課程?

❸ How do I enroll in ESL classes?
我要怎麼報名 ESL 的課程?

❹ What do I need to bring to register?
我需要帶什麼資料去註冊嗎？

❹ How long have you offered ESL classes?
你們提供 ESL 課程已經幾年了？

❻ How many students are in the ESL program?
ESL 課程中有多少學生？

Unit

45

MP3-46

Asking for Information
詢問相關資料

 情境對話

A Hello. I'm calling to find out information about the school.
嗨，我想問一些有關學校的資料。

B Sure. What would you like to know?
好的，你想要什麼樣的資料呢？

A Do my children need to be tested for placement before enrolling?
我的小孩在入學前需要經過分班測試嗎？

B Yes. I can make an appointment for you.
是的，我可以幫您預約。

How old are they?
他們多大了？

A My daughter is thirteen, and my son is fifteen.
我女兒 13 歲、兒子 15 歲。

B Have they gone to school in the United States before?
他們以前在美國上過學嗎？

A No.
沒有。

例句隨身包

❶ I need to find out the number for the local school.
我想要知道本地學校的電話號碼。

❷ Do my children need to be tested before enrolling?
我的小孩在入學前需要經過分班測試嗎？

❸ How do I enroll?
我要如何才能入學？

❹ Is there an address I can mail their records to?

我要把他們的就學記錄寄到哪裡呢？

❹ Which school is close by, and where exactly is it located?

哪一家學校比較近，該校確切位置在哪裡？

❻ Is there a dress code?

有沒有服裝規定？

❼ Is there a bus system?

有沒有校車系統？

❽ When is the first day of school, and how long is the school year?

開學日是哪天，學年有多長？

❾ How much are school lunches?

學校午餐收費多少？

46

MP3-47

Asking about Application Procedures
詢問申請程序

情境對話

A I need to enroll my child in school.
我需要送我小孩入學。

We just moved to the country.
我們剛剛搬來這個國家。

B Do you have a birth certificate and shot records?
你有孩子們的出生證明和預防針記錄嗎？

A Yes. Do I need to bring those with me?
有，我需要帶它們過去嗎？

B Yes. We will need those when you fill out the application for enrollment.
是的，當您填入學表格時，我們會需要這些資料。

A Can I come tomorrow?
　我明天可以過來嗎？

B Yes. Come to the main office anytime between the hours of 8:00 a.m. and 4:30 p.m.
　可以，明天八點到四點半之間，您都可以到我們的總辦公室來。

例句隨身包

❶ What do I need to bring with me to enroll?
我辦理入學手續時，需要什麼資料？

❷ Have you received my children's records from their prior school?
你有沒有收到我小孩之前就讀學校寄給你的就學記錄？

❸ What are the results of the placement tests?
分班考試結果如何？

④ Do you have separate forms for ESL classes?

ESL 課程有沒有另外的表格？

⑤ What if we don't have a birth certificate or shot records?

如果我們沒有出生證明或預防針記錄，應該要怎麼辦？

⑥ What information do you need to finish the paperwork?

需要什麼資料才能完成文件手續？

Unit
47

MP3-48

First Day of School
開學的第一天

情境對話

A What time does he need to be there in the morning?
他早上幾點要到學校？

B At eight o'clock.
八點鐘。

A Does he need to bring any supplies?
他需要帶任何文具用品嗎？

B No. Not today.
不用，開學日不用。

The teacher will give him a list of school supplies.
老師會給他一個文具用品表。

A Okay. I've arranged for the daycare center to pick him up after his classes are over.

好的，我已經安排好安親班的人在下課會去接他。

What time should I tell them to pick him up?

我應該告訴他們幾點去接人呢？

B Kindergarten is only half-day, so tell them to come by at noon.

幼稚園只有半天課，叫他們中午過來接人吧。

例句隨身包

❶ Where does my daughter need to go?
我女兒應該要去哪裡？

❷ What time do classes begin?
課幾點開始？

❸ What supplies will be needed?
需要帶什麼文具用品？

4 Is all the paperwork finished?
所有文書手續都完成了嗎？

5 Will my child have someone there to help him with his English?
會不會有人提供我孩子英文方面的協助？

6 Do we need to buy books, or will they be provided?
我們需要買書或學校會提供書？

7 What time do I need to pick her up after school?
我下課時應該幾點去接她？

8 I will drop her off at school, but my neighbor will be picking her up.
我會載她上學，但我鄰居會去接她下課。

Do I need to tell anyone or sign any papers?
我需要通知任何人或簽署任何文件嗎？

Parent-Teacher Conference
親師懇談會

情境對話

A Hello, Mrs. Smith. I'm Mr. Lewis, your son's teacher.

嗨，史密斯太太，我是你兒子的老師，名叫路易斯。

B Well, hello. Is there a problem at school?

嗨，他在學校不乖嗎？

A Not really. I just thought we might schedule a conference.

不是這樣的，我只是想安排個時間，讓我們碰個面。

B Why do we need to have a conference if there's not a problem?

如果沒有什麼問題，為什麼需要開會？

His grades have dropped a little, but my husband and I talked with him about it.

他的成績有些退步，但我和先生已經和他溝通過。

A His grades are fine.

他的成績不是問題。

It's just that he seems to be having trouble with some of his classmates, and I thought we should talk about some things.

他似乎和班上有些同學處不來，還有一些事我認為我們應該談談。

B Okay. Would Friday afternoon be convenient for you?

好的，星期五下午你方便嗎？

A Perfect. About 3:30.

很好，那三點半碰面吧。

例句隨身包

❶ I was wondering how my son is doing in class.

我想知道我兒子在學校表現如何。

Can we schedule a conference for 4:30 on Wednesday?
我們可以安排星期三四點半時見面談談。

❷ Why do we need to have a conference?
我們為什麼需要開會談談？

Is there a problem with my daughter?
我女兒有什麼問題嗎？

❸ How are his grades?
他的成績如何？

❹ I need to schedule a conference about his last test.
我需要為他上次考試成績和您碰個面。

❺ I'm not going to be able to make it on Wednesday.
我星期三沒空。

Can we reschedule for next Monday?
可以換到下週一嗎？

6 My son seems to be having problems in school.
我兒子似乎在學校碰上些麻煩。

I'd like to talk about it if you have time.
如果你有時間,我想和你談談。

7 Do you think my daughter is adjusting well to the school?
你認為我女兒在學校適應的好嗎?

notes

Chapter **8**

求職英語

英語已是職場上的最佳利器，做好準備，主動出擊，才能輕鬆掌握職缺訊息；充實英語能力，才能有效爭取合理的薪資福利。

49

MP3-50

Looking for a Job
找工作

情境對話

A Hello.
嗨。

B Hi. My name is Sara and I am calling about your job opening.
嗨，我叫莎拉，想問一下你們的空缺。

A We are looking for someone to work part-time at the register.
我們在找一個兼職的結帳人員。

B Can I come in today and pick up an application?
我今天可以過來拿一份申請單嗎？

A If you're interested, we can schedule you for an interview.
如果你有興趣的話，我們可以幫你安排個面試。

B That would be great. When would it be convenient for me to come in?
太好了，我什麼時候可以過來呢？

例句隨身包

❶ Can you tell me if there is a job opening?
你可以告訴我目前是否有空缺嗎？

❷ Excuse me. Can you tell me if you are accepting applications?
抱歉，能否告訴我你們現在有接受申請嗎？

❸ I saw your ad in the newspaper.
我看到你們在報上登的廣告。

Can you tell me where I can apply?
能否告訴我要到哪裡申請？

❹ Are you still looking for full-time workers?
你們仍然在徵全職人員嗎？

❺ Has the employment position already been filled?
工作空缺已經找到人了嗎？

❻ I saw that you were hiring.
我看到你們在徵人。

❼ Can you tell me about your employment opportunities?
能否告訴我你們這裡的工作機會。

Unit

50

MP3-51

Applying for a Job
申請工作

情境對話

A I am here to apply for a job.
我是來申請工作的

Can I have an application?
能不能給我一份申請表？

B Yes. I have one right here.
好的，我這裡剛好有一份。

A Thank you. Can you tell me if there are any specific requirements for the job?
謝謝，能否告訴我這份工作有沒有任何特殊條件？

B Job experience is helpful.
有過工作經驗會有幫助。

A Do I just fill out my application here and leave it with you?

我只要把申請表填好，留給你就可以了嗎？

B Yes. We should get back to you shortly.

是的，我們會盡快給你回音。

例句隨身包

❶ Can you tell me if there are any job opportunities?

能否告訴我你們這裡有沒有工作機會？

❷ I need information on the job openings here.

我需要這裡工作空缺的一些資料。

❸ I am applying for a job here.

我想申請這裡的工作。

Do I need a resume?

我需要帶一份履歷表嗎？

4 What are the skills required for the job?
這份工作需要什麼樣的技巧？

5 What is the salary range for this job?
這份工作的薪水大約如何？

6 Is the job opening available full-time only?
這個工作空缺是不是只有全職的？

7 Can I make an appointment for an interview today?
我可以安排今天的面試嗎？

8 Is a specific degree required?
這工作有要求特殊學歷嗎？

181

Unit

51

MP3-52

Filling out a Job Application
填工作申請表

情境對話

A Can I help you, sir?

先生，有什麼我可以幫您的嗎？

B Yes. I need to fill out an application.

是的，我需要填申請表。

A Here you are.

這裡有一份。

You can either sit here and fill it out or bring it back to us another day.

你可以坐在這裡填表或改天再把申請表送過來。

B Thank you. Can you tell me when the position is going to be filled?

謝謝，你能否告訴我這個工作的申請何時截止？

A At the end of this month.
這個月底。

B Thank you very much for your help.
謝謝你的協助。

例句隨身包

❶ I am here to fill out an application.
我是來填申請表的。

Can you tell me where to go?
可以告訴我要到哪裡去嗎？

❷ Can you tell me when the position will be filled?
能否告訴我這個工作的申請何時截止？

❸ Do I fill out my social security number here?
我應該把社會安全號碼填在這裡嗎？

4 Do you need my phone number and address?

你需要我的電話號碼和住址嗎？

5 Should I mail in my application?

我應該將申請表格用寄的嗎？

6 How long will you be accepting applications?

你們會接受申請到什麼時候為止？

7 Should I include my previous salary?

我應該要提及我前任工作的薪資資料嗎？

8 Do you need my previous work experience?

你需要我之前工作的經驗嗎？

Unit

52

MP3-53

Job Interview
工作面試

情境對話

A I have an appointment with Mr. Tran for a job interview.

我和特安先生安排了工作面試。

B He will be right with you.

他馬上就過來。

Did you bring your resume?

你有帶履歷表來嗎？

A I have my references, previous work history, and a recommendation.

我帶來了一些查詢資料、之前的工作紀錄和推薦信。

Is there anything else I need?

我還要帶別的文件嗎？

B No. He can see you now in his office.
不用，他現在在辦公室等你了。

A Thank you.
謝謝。

例句隨身包

❶ Here is a list of my previous work experience.
這是我以前的工作經驗。

❷ I wrote down my references' addresses.
我寫下了推薦人的地址。

Do you need their phone numbers also?
你需要他們的電話號碼嗎？

❸ I have a degree in business.
我有商業學歷。

❹ I graduated from the University of Dallas.
我畢業於達拉斯大學。

5 I am only looking for a part-time job right now.
我現在要找的只是兼職工作。

6 I am looking for a company with health care.
我要找有提供健保的公司。

7 I am hoping to gain the vital skills that I need from this job opportunity.
我希望能從這個工作機會中，學到我所需要的重要技巧。

8 Will I be making about the same salary as my previous job?
我的薪水會和前一份工作一樣多嗎？

Unit

53

MP3-54

Negotiating Salary
討論薪資

情境對話

A Now, it's time to talk salary.
현現在，讓我們來討論一下薪資吧。

I see you were making $12 an hour at your last employment.
我知道你在上一份工作中，每個小時賺 12 元美金。

B Yes, plus some benefits.
是的，還有一些福利。

A I see. Well, here the position pays only $10 an hour, but there are full benefits.
我懂了，這份工作一小時只有 10 元美金，但我們提供全套福利。

B Is there any chance for evaluation of performance with raises?
未來有沒有機會透過工作評估得到加薪呢？

A Yes. Every six months, all employees are evaluated and raises are given based on that.
有的，每六個月會評估一次，是否加薪要看評估結果。

例句隨身包

❶ I was making ten dollars an hour.
我一小時賺十元。

What is your company planning to pay?
你們公司打算付多少錢呢？

❷ What is the current salary of your employees?
你現在的雇員都領多少薪水呢？

❸ What are you willing to pay for the job?
你願意支付多少錢給這份工作呢？

4 I am hoping to make thirty thousand dollars a year.
我希望一年能夠賺 3 萬美金。

5 I believe my skills and experience are worth more than that.
我相信我的技能和經驗值得更高的薪資。

6 If I take the promotion, it will require moving my family to a new city.
如果我接受這個升遷，我和家人就得搬到另一個城市去。

Is the salary going to be worth it?
新的薪水值得我們這麼做嗎？

7 I'm being offered more money by a competitive firm.
另一家競爭公司提供我更高的薪水。

Are you willing to match their offer?
你們公司願意和他們提供一樣的薪水嗎？

Chapter 9

投資理財

買賣股票、選擇優良的投資理財顧問和創業伙伴,商業英語學習,能夠助你快速取得金融資訊、達成投資交易、尋找合適的商業伙伴。

Investment
投資

情境對話

A I'm looking for someone to help me invest some money.

我正在找尋可以幫助我投資的人。

Do you know anyone?

你認識這樣的人嗎？

B My cousin is an investment advisor.

我表哥是投資顧問。

I can give you his number.

我可以把他的電話號碼給你。

A That would be great.

太好了。

Is he a CPA or a securities broker?

他是合格的會計師還是證券經紀人？

B I'm not sure.
我不太確定。

A Well, what kind of investment instruments does he deal with?
他處理什麼樣的投資工具？

B I don't know. Just call him.
我不知道。打電話問他吧。

A He is licensed, isn't he?
他領有執照，對吧。

例句隨身包

❶ Who do I need to talk to about investments?
關於投資，我應該找誰？

❷ Does this bank handle investments?
這家銀行可以處理投資事宜嗎？

❸ If I wanted to speak to someone about what kind of investment instruments are available, where would I need to go?
如果我想要和某人談談，以便瞭解我可以選擇的投資工具，我應該要到哪裡呢？

❹ What is a limited mutual fund?
什麼是限制共同基金？

❹ What about stocks?
那股票呢？

❻ Do you invest?
你投資嗎？
Who do you go through?
你透過誰進行投資？

❼ I'm looking for an investment advisor. Know anyone?
我想找一個投資顧問，你有認識的人嗎？

❽ Are you a CPA?
你是會計師嗎？

❾ Are you licensed?
你有合格執照嗎？

Unit

55

MP3-56

Stocks
買賣股票

情境對話

A Look at the stock market today.
看看今天的股市。

B Is it bad?
很不好嗎？

A No, it's reaching an all time high.
不，今天股市創新高。

B What does that mean—buy or sell?
那是什麼意思？是買壓還是賣壓？

A In the stock market, you want to buy low and sell high.
在股市裡，人們想要買低賣高。

B Oh, I guess you need to call your stockbroker then.

噢，我想你需要打電話給你的股票經紀人。

A Already did.

我已經打過了

❶ Did you see the stock report today?
你看到今天的股票報告了沒？

It looks like it's time to sell.
看樣子，賣股票的時刻到了。

❷ The Dow Jones has had an amazing rise and fall in the last month.
道瓊指數在上個月起伏多次。

Are you doing okay?
你沒有受到什麼影響吧？

❸ Did you call your broker to buy that stock?
你有打電話給你的經紀人說要買那支股票嗎？

I heard it's on the rise.
我聽說它正在漲。

❹ I made a great profit.
我賺了一筆。

I bought low and sold high.
我買低賣高。

❺ Can you tell me how you knew to buy that stock?
你能否告訴我，你怎麼知道該買那支股票？

Unit

56

MP3-57

Buying Mutual funds, Bonds
買共同基金、債券

情境對話

A Can I help you?

我可以為你效勞嗎？

B Yes, I'm looking into buying a mutual fund or bond or something like that, but I'm not sure what each offers.

是的，我考慮要買共同基金、公債或類似的投資，但我不確定它們有什麼不同的地方。

A Would you like to see some information about our banking opportunities?

你想要看看我們銀行可以提供哪些理財方式嗎？

B Yes, please. If I have any questions about this, whom would I need to contact?

是的，如果我有任何疑問的話，我應該和誰聯絡？

A I believe a direct number to investments is right at the bottom, and we can handle everything right here in this bank.

我想資料的正下方有一個你可以直接聯絡的投資專線，我們可以直接在銀行處理所有事宜。

B Great. Thank you for your help.

太好了，謝謝你的協助。

❶ I would like to invest my money, but I'm not sure if I want mutual funds or bonds.

我想要投資，但我不確定我想投資共同基金或公債。

Whom should I talk to?

我該和誰談呢？

❷ Do you know anything about getting into CDs or special banking products?

你知道要如何進行大額可轉讓定存或特殊銀行產品嗎？

❸ What is the advantage of a special savings deposit?

特殊定存的好處是什麼？

❹ How do I know the difference in mutual funds?

我怎麼知道共同基金有哪些不同？

❺ What exactly does your bank offer?

你的銀行到底提供哪些投資選擇？

Unit

57

MP3-58

Looking for a Business Partner
找尋商業伙伴

情境對話

A I heard you are starting up your own business.
我聽說你正要創業。

B Trying to. I'm having a little trouble.
我嘗試要這麼做，但有一些問題。

A Really? I thought you had it all worked out.
真的嗎？我以為一切都很順利。

B I did until one of my business partners pulled out.
原本很順利，直到一位商業伙伴決定抽手。

Now, I'm short on capital for the business, so I'm looking for a new partner to help invest some money.
現在，我的資本不夠，所以我正在找新伙伴來幫忙投資。

A Any luck finding someone?

找到任何人了嗎？

B Sort of. Why? Are you interested?

好像吧，為什麼？你有興趣嗎？

例句隨身包

❶ I wanted to set up a small business but I'm not sure I want to go in alone.

我想要成立小公司，但我不確定我想要一個人做。

Do you know anyone who is looking for a business partner?

你知道有人在找生意伙伴嗎？

❷ We've spent too much time working in this store.

我們花了太多的時間在這家店上。

I think we could start a great store of our own.

我認為我們應該自己開店。

What do you say to going into business together?
你覺得一起開店這個主意如何？

❸ I think if we combined our assets, we would be even more successful.
我認為如果我們結合彼此的財產，我們可能會更成功。

What do you think about being partners?
你覺得我們做伙伴如何？

❹ My brother-in-law is having financial troubles, so I invited him to move up here and be my business partner.
我大舅子有財務困難，所以我邀請他搬到這裡來當我的生意伙伴。

Buying a Business
購買一個企業

情境對話

A I heard the restaurant is up for sale.
我聽說這家餐廳要頂讓。

B Yes. I'm moving.
對，我要搬家了。

A How was business?
生意如何？

B Really great, but my mother's sick, and I have
to be with her.
很棒，但我媽生病了，我必須照顧她。

Are you interested in buying it?
你想要買下這家餐廳嗎？

A I've been thinking about it.
我一直在考慮。

I just need to get some capital together and possibly some business partners.
我只需要籌一些資金，如果可能的話，再找一些生意伙伴。

B Well, give me call, and we'll talk.
這樣吧，打電話給我，我們可以談談。

例句隨身包

❶ I heard the shoe store at the end of the street is going out of business.
我聽說街角的那家鞋店要停業了。

I wonder if the store itself is for sale.
我好奇那家店會不會出售。

❷ I'd like to invest my money in your business.
我想把錢投資在你的生意上。

❸ What exactly is your offer?
你的提議到底是什麼？

❹ Do you have enough capital to buy a business?

你有足夠的資金，來買下一家店嗎？

❺ What kind of business are you interested in?

你對什麼生意有興趣？

❻ How do I go about getting a loan to start a business?

我要怎樣申請貸款來自己開業呢？

Chapter **10**

求救！

生活中無可避免的是意外，
「S.O.S！」是隨身必攜的錦囊妙
藥。

Unit

59

MP3-60

Being Lost in Town
在城裡迷路時

情境對話

A Sorry to bother you.
抱歉打擾你。

Can you help my family find the Ft. Worth stockyards?
你能否幫我家人找到福和市的牲畜飼養場？

B Do you know what street it's on?
你知道它在哪條街上嗎？

A It is here on this map.
在地圖上的這裡。

B Look for the street signs on every corner.
在每個街角，仔細看每條街名。

It should be about two blocks from here.
應該離這裡只有兩條街遠。

A Do I keep going north?
我需要一直往北走嗎？

B Yes. Two miles up the road.
是的，往北走兩英里。

例句隨身包

❶ I am lost. How do I get back on the highway?
我迷路了，要怎麼才能回到高速公路上？

❷ Can I buy a map anywhere?
我可以去哪裡買地圖呢？

❸ How do I get back to where I came from?
我要怎麼回到我原來的地方？

❹ Where are the residential streets?
住宅區在哪裡？

❺ Do you know how to get to the Wild Flower Festival in Richardson?
你知道要如何去李察遜市的野花慶典嗎？

❻ Excuse me, sir. Where can I buy a map?
先生，抱歉。我可以在哪裡買到地圖？

❼ How do I get to this town?
我要如何去這個鎮？

❽ How far am I from this highway?
我離這條高速公路有多遠？

Unit

60

MP3-61

Asking for Directions
問方向

A　Are you lost?
　　你迷路了嗎？

B　Yes. I am looking for Huntington Avenue.
　　是的，我在找杭廷頓大道。

A　In Plano?
　　布南諾市的杭廷頓大道？

B　Yes. Can you give me directions?
　　是的，你能告訴我怎麼去嗎？

A　It's a good ten miles south of here.
　　那裡離這裡至少要向南開十英里。

B I just need to find Shellstone Street again and then I'll be set.

我只需要找到貝石街，之後就沒問題了。

❶ I am looking for 156 Elm Street.
我正在找艾姆街 156 號。

Can you tell me how to get there?
你能否告訴我要怎麼走？

❷ I need to find Tulip Circle.
我需要找到鬱金香圓環。

Can you help me?
你能否幫我？

❸ I need to get back to Pearl Trails.
我需要回到珍珠大道。

Do you have a map?
你有地圖嗎？

4 Do you have a phone I can borrow?
我可以借用你的電話嗎？

I need to call and get directions to Victor Avenue.
我要打電話去問，怎麼去維多大道。

5 I am lost. Can you help me get back on the highway?
我迷路了，你能否告訴我要如何回到高速公路上？

6 I don't know how I got off the major roads. Can you help?
我不知道自己是怎麼離開主要道路的，你能幫我嗎？

7 Do you know the way to downtown Dallas?
你知道要怎麼去達拉斯市中心嗎？

8 Can you give me directions to the mall?
你能告訴我去購物中心的方向嗎？

61

MP3-62

Involved in a Car Accident
碰上了車禍

情境對話

A Are you hurt?
你受傷了嗎？

I am sorry.
我很抱歉。

I didn't see you turning.
我沒看見你轉彎。

B No, I am fine. Are you all right?
我沒事，你還好嗎？

A I'm fine. I was wearing my seatbelt.
我很好，我有繫安全帶。

Is there any damage done to your car?
你的車有沒有損傷？

B　I don't think so but I would like to get your insurance number and other information just in case.
我想沒有，但我想向你要你的保險單號碼和其他資料，以防萬一。

A　Sure. If there is a problem, you can just call my insurance company.
沒問題，如果有任何問題，你可以聯絡我的保險公司。

B　There doesn't seem to be any problem, but it's better to be safe than sorry.
目前似乎沒什麼問題，但還是小心一點比較好。

例句隨身包

❶ Are you hurt?
你有受傷嗎？

❷ I need an ambulance.
我需要叫救護車。

I think my leg is broken.
我想我的腿斷了。

❸ Can we settle this, or do we need a police officer?

我們能否私下和解，還是需要找警察？

❹ Do you have insurance?

你有保險嗎？

❺ Can I have your insurance number?

我可以向你要保險單號碼嗎？

❻ Let me get your license plate number and phone number.

讓我抄下你的車牌號碼和電話號碼。

❼ Are you sure you are not hurt?

你確定你沒受傷？

Do you need to go the emergency room?

你需要去急診室嗎？

❽ What damage was done to your car?

你的車有什麼損傷嗎？

Unit

62

Injury
受傷

MP3-63

情境對話

A Keri fell on the sidewalk and hit her head.
凱莉在人行道上跌倒，撞到了頭。

B Is she bleeding?
她有流血嗎？

A Yes. I think she will need stitches.
有，我想她可能需要縫幾針。

B Should we take her to her doctor or to the emergency room?
我們應該帶她去看她的醫生，還是送她去急診室？

A Call her doctor and see if he is available.
打電話給她的醫生，看看他有沒有空。

The bleeding hasn't stopped.

血還沒止住呢。

B Go help her in the car while I call her doctor.

我打電話給她的醫生，你到車上去看著她。

例句隨身包

1 I cut my finger on the can opener.

我的手指不小心被開罐器割到。

I think I need stitches.

我想我需要縫個幾針。

❷ Can you move your arm?

你可以移動手臂嗎？

You may have broken it.

你的手可能斷了。

❸ I can tell your finger is broken.

我看得出來你的手指斷了。

❹ I think we are going to take you to the doctor.

我想我們需要送你去看醫生。

Glass shards may be deeply embedded in the wound.
玻璃碎片可能會深深嵌入傷口裡。

❹ Should I call the ambulance, or do you think you can walk?
我應該叫救護車嗎，你認為自己還可以走路嗎？

❻ Those burns on your hand are bad.
你手上的這些燙傷很糟糕。
We need to go to the emergency room.
我們需要去急診室。

❼ I have already called an ambulance.
我已經叫了救護車。

Put pressure on the cut with this towel.
用這條毛巾壓在傷口上。

❽ You were hit in the head with a baseball bat.
你被球棒打到頭了。

We'd better take you to the emergency room.
我們最好把你送到急診室去。

63

MP3-64

Calling for Emergency Help
求助急診

情境對話

A I heard there was a bomb threat at the high school today.

我聽說高中今天接到了炸彈威脅？

B Yes.

是的。

A Did they call the police?

他們報警了嗎？

B Yes. Everyone had to leave the building.

是的，每個人都必須離開大樓。

A They didn't find anything I hope.

我希望他們沒有找到任何東西。

B No. It seems to have been nothing more than a joke, but I am glad they called 911.

沒有，這整件事似乎只是個玩笑，但我很高興他們還是打電話報警了。

 例句隨身包

❶ Call 911. Katie is missing.
打電話報警，凱蒂不見了。

❷ We need an ambulance.
我們需要救護車。
Jack was hit by a car.
傑克被車撞了。

❸ There is a fire next door.
隔壁失火了。
Call the fire department.
打電話給消防隊。

❹ In case of an emergency, the police and fire departments should always stay by the phone.
當緊急狀況發生時，警方和消防隊都應該在電話旁待命。

❺ There is a gun fight down the street.
街尾發生了槍戰。

I think you should call the police.
我想你應該報警。

❻ Get the paramedics.
找醫護人員。

The Miller's two-year-old was found unconscious in the pool.
米勒家兩歲的孩子掉到游泳池裡，救起來時已經昏迷。

❼ We'd better call the fire department. I smell smoke.
我們最好打電話給消防隊，我聞到煙味了。

❽ I think Billy was kidnapped.
我認為比利被綁架了。

We'd better call the police.
我們最好報警。

❾ I guess it was just a false alarm, but I am glad we called 911.
我想這是假警報，但還是很高興我們報了警。

Unit

64

MP3-65

Someone Broke in
家裡被偷了

A   The window out back was broken.
後面通往外面的窗戶被打破了。

That is how they got in.
他們就是這樣進來的。

B   So many break-ins occur around Christmas time.
許多偷竊案發生在聖誕節。

A   That is why alarms are useful.
這就是警報器的功用了。

We are also going to get a dog.
我們也即將要買一隻狗。

B   You can never be too safe.
安全決沒有嫌多的時候。

223

A I am just glad that nobody was hurt.
我只是很高興沒人受傷。

B Next time you go on vacation, make sure someone collects your mail and newspaper, so people won't know you're gone.
下次你去度假時，要確定有人幫你收信、拿報紙，所以別人才不會知道你不在。

例句隨身包

❶ I hear our neighbor's huuse alarm.
我聽到鄰居的警報響了。
We'd better call the police.
我們最好報警。

❷ When I saw the back door wide open, I immediately called the police.
當我看到後門大開時，我立刻就報警了。

❸ Go next door, and call the police.
去隔壁報警。

Someone broke in through the bedroom window.
有人從臥室的窗戶進入我們家了。

4 No one saw the thief, but someone stole everything valuable in the middle of the night.
沒有人看見小偷，但有人在午夜把每件珍貴東西都偷走了。

5 While the Henderson's were on vacation, a burglar broke into their house.
當杭德生一家人去度假時，小偷闖進他們家偷竊。

6 I think we should get an alarm.
我認為我們應該裝警報器。
It isn't safe being home alone.
一個人在家不安全。

7 Call the police, and tell them someone is trying to break in.
去報警告訴他們有人想要闖入我們家行竊。

8 Car theft is very common.
偷車事件很常見。

That is why many people have car alarms.
因此許多人都裝有車子的警報器。

Unit

65

MP3-66

Seeking Police Assistance

尋求警察協助

情境對話

A What happened to you?
你怎麼了嗎？

B Can you call the police, sir?
先生，麻煩請你報警。

Someone attacked me and stole my purse.
某個人攻擊了我，偷了我的錢包。

A Do you need an ambulance?
你需要救護車嗎？

That cut on your face looks bad.
你臉上的割傷看起來很嚴重。

B No, I am fine.
不，我沒事。

I should report this incident to the police.
我應該將這件意外通報警方。

A They are on their way.
他們正在來的路上。

Just sit down, and I will get you some coffee.
先坐下，我幫你倒杯咖啡。

B Thank you, sir.
先生，謝謝你。

例句隨身包

❶ I need police assistance.
我需要警察協助。

Someone is following me.
有人在跟蹤我。

❷ A man just robbed me.
有個人剛剛搶了我。

Call the police.
請打電話報警。

❸ A man is assaulting that lady over there.
那邊有個男人正在攻擊一位女士。

I think we'd better call the police.
我想我們最好報警。

❹ That party next door is very loud and it is late.
隔壁的舞會很吵,而且現在也很晚了。

I think we should call the police.
我想我們應該報警。

❺ That wreck looks bad.
那個車禍看起來蠻嚴重的。

We should call the police.
我們應該報警。

❻ I found this little girl crying.
我發現這個哭泣的小女孩。

We should call for police assistance.
我們應該報警尋求協助。

❼ The car won't start and it is late.
車子發不動，而且已經很晚了。

Maybe we should call for police assistance.
也許我們應該報警尋求協助。

❽ If that man stole any merchandise, we should call the police immediately.
如果那個男人偷竊任何商品，我們就應該立刻報警。

There are tracts in my life that are bare and silent.
They are the open spaces where my busy days had their light and air.

-Rabindranath Tagore

在我生命中有許多廣闊、寂靜之地。

這些空曠的地方，為我忙碌的日子，提供陽光和空氣。

—泰戈爾

66

MP3-67

Being Locked out of the House
被鎖在門外

情境對話

A My kids have lost their house keys again.
我的小孩又把家裡的鑰匙弄丟了。

B Isn't that their third time losing them?
這不是第三次了嗎？

A I'd better go home and let them in.
我最好回家去幫他們開門。

B Why don't you make them a chain with the house key on it so they can wear it around their necks?
你為什麼不幫他們準備鑰匙環呢？這樣他們就可以把鑰匙帶在脖子上了。

A That is a good idea. Maybe I should try it.

那主意不錯，也許我應該試試看。

B That way they can't lose their keys again.

這樣一來，他們就不會再把鑰匙弄丟了。

例句隨身包

❶ Can I use your phone?

我可以借你的電話用嗎？

I am locked out of my house.

我被鎖在門外了。

❷ Do you know the locksmith's number?

你知道鎖匠的電話號碼嗎？

I locked my keys in my car.

我把車鑰匙鎖在車裡了。

❸ I lost the keys to my house.

我把家裡的鑰匙弄丟了。

Can you help me climb into that open window?

你可以幫我一把，讓我爬進那個打開的窗戶嗎？

❹ I am locked out.

我被鎖在門外了。

Can I call my wife from your phone?

可以用你的電話，打電話給我太太嗎？

❺ I have lost my keys.

我把鑰匙弄丟了。

Can I call a locksmith from your office?

我可以從你辦公室打電話叫鎖匠嗎？

❻ Can you call security?

你可以打電話叫警衛嗎？

I have lost my keys.

我弄丟我的鑰匙了。

❼ Can I get a replacement key?

我可以再打一份鑰匙嗎？

I seemed to have lost my keys.

我好像把鑰匙弄丟了。

❽ I lost my house keys.

我遺失了家裡的鑰匙。

Can we change our locks?

我們可以換鎖嗎？

notes

英語系列：56

7天學好流利英語會話

作者／施孝昌
出版者／哈福企業有限公司
地址／新北市板橋區五權街 16 號
電話／(02)2808-6545　傳真／(02) 2808-6545
郵政劃撥／ 31598840　戶名／哈福企業有限公司
出版日期／ 2019 年 4 月
定價／ NT$ 299 元 (附 MP3)

全球華文國際市場總代理／采舍國際有限公司
地址／新北市中和區中山路 2 段 366 巷 10 號 3 樓
電話／(02) 8245-8786　傳真／(02) 8245-8718
網址／ www.silkbook.com　新絲路華文網

香港澳門總經銷／和平圖書有限公司
地址／香港柴灣嘉業街 12 號百樂門大廈 17 樓
電話／(852) 2804-6687 傳真／(852) 2804-6409
定價／港幣 100 元 (附 MP3)

email ／ haanet68@Gmail.com

郵撥打九折，郵撥未滿 500 元，酌收 1 成運費，
滿 500 元以上者免運費

國家圖書館出版品預行編目資料

7天學好流利英語會話 / 施孝昌著. -- 新北市：哈福
企業, 2019.04
　面；　公分. -- (英語系列；56)
　ISBN 978-986-97425-2-8(平裝附光碟片)

1.英語 2.會話

805.188　　　　　　　　　　　108004760

哈福

哈福